"Aren't you the least bit leery of hitting on a woman in a wedding gown?

"This dress has commitment written all over it, and I'd bet the ranch that you're the kind of guy who starts singing 'Don't Fence Me In' after the second date. You don't scare me, Ben. I had you pegged long before I invited you to climb into this van with me. Now, be the nice guy that you really are and unbutton the dress."

"You think you've got me all figured out, don't you, Sara?"

"Look, Ben, I just need your body for a few hours. That's all. The rest is incidental. Now, would you please slip in behind me and start unbuttoning."

"Wouldn't it be easier to pull over and actually stop the vehicle?"

"My entire future hinges on what happens tonight, and I am not going to arrive late. Now, there's plenty of room, so just throw your leg over, straddle the seat and ease your way down."

"You're the boss," Ben said, wondering—not for the first time—just what he was getting himself into with this bold and beautiful bride.

Dear Reader,

Magic, like love, is in the eye of the beholder. So who's to say that magic, along with love, can't be stitched into the seams of a wedding dress...an antique gown that changes the lives of three special brides and their unsuspecting bridegrooms. I imagined just such a dress and the trouble that might follow if it was mistakenly delivered to a practical, plan-your-work-and-work-your-plan kind of lady. When the magic wedding dress *twinkles* at Sara Gunnerson and sends her crashing into the arms of Ben Northcross, trouble is exactly what occurs in *The Fifty-Cent Groom*.

Daydreamer that I am, I believe it could happen and, as you read Sara and Ben's story, I hope you will believe it, too. After all, isn't there a touch of magic, a gentle twist of fate, any time a man and woman fall in love?

Karen Toller Whittenburg

Karen Toller Whittenburg

THE FIFTY-CENT GROOM

Harlequin Books

TORONTO • NEW YORK • LONDON
AMSTERDAM • PARIS • SYDNEY • HAMBURG
STOCKHOLM • ATHENS • TOKYO • MILAN
MADRID • WARSAW • BUDAPEST • AUCKLAND

ISBN 0-373-16630-3

THE FIFTY-CENT GROOM

Chapter One

If the dress hadn't twinkled at her, Sara Gunnerson never would have put it on.

In all her twenty-eight years, she had never done anything so foolish, so completely impulsive. But from the moment her brother had carried it into the house, she had been drawn to the antique wedding gown like a bee to a blossom.

It was obvious, of course, that the dress was wrong from hem to veil. It was not the gown she'd sent Jason to pick up at the dry cleaners. And it definitely was not the sleek, slim-skirted bridal ensemble she was supposed to deliver to the church on Saturday. If she showed up with *this* dress, tomorrow's wedding would very likely be the last she was hired to coordinate.

And even knowing that, she had stood staring—smiling, actually—at the dress. Lost in some kind of daydream, bound by some kind of spell.

She had talked to Jason, fussed at him for not noticing the mistake, listened to his ever-ready excuses and heard him say he hadn't even looked at the dress, that he had just accepted what the clerk at the Starz Laundry and Dry Cleaners handed him. How was he to have known it wasn't the wedding gown Sara had sent him to pick up? What did he know about brides and what they wore? With all the pickups and deliveries she'd given him to do that day, when had he had time to look at a stupid wedding dress? If she didn't like the way he did things, why didn't she do it all herself?

He'd slammed the door on his way out, and she hadn't shifted her attention from the dress long enough to have the last word.

Not that it was the most beautiful bridal gown she'd ever set eyes on. It wasn't. And not that it was the kind of dress she had dreamed of wearing someday. It wasn't that, either. But she couldn't stay away from it, and even after she hung it in her bedroom, she kept wandering back there to stand staring at the heavy satin and richly detailed lace, the delicate stitching and the tiny buttons on the sleeves and down the back.

When the clerk from Starz called to apologize profusely for her mistake and to make arrangements for an employee to pick up the gown, Sara sank onto the mattress in a stifling wave of disappointment. Sitting cross-legged on her bed, she had stared at the dress, vaguely aware that she had last-minute preparations to make for tonight's party but oddly unconcerned by the passage of time. It was a curious sensation to be entranced by a few yards of fabric, and she couldn't begin to explain her compulsion. Still, she sat and stared and sighed.

Then the dress had twinkled—just like Dudley Do-Right's smile—and inspiration had seized her. If West Ridgeman could see her in the dress, he would realize she was the love of his life and propose on the spot. It seemed a perfectly brilliant idea, and the next thing she knew, her ultra-chic, ultra-refined party dress was an unsophisticated lump on the floor and she was up to her neck in satin and lace.

No sooner had she fastened the last tiny button, smoothed the lace scallops at her wrists, set the bridal veil haphazardly on her head and turned to look in the mirror than the spell burst like a bubble. She stared at her reflection, amazed at what she had done, astounded that she had thought putting on this gown was an intelligent idea.

Not only was it an inexplicable error in judgment, but it wasn't even a dress she would consider for her own wedding. She had always planned to float down the aisle in a pure white gown of raw silk and seed pearls, something contemporary and elegant and excruciatingly expensive.

Certainly nothing as simple and old-fashioned as this gown. Nothing so reminiscent of blushing brides and bridegrooms. But despite her preconceptions, the wedding dress was vastly becoming, complementing her auburn hair with the color of candlelight, draping her slenderness in the soft whisk of satin.

With uncharacteristic fussiness, she smoothed the front of the gown, liking the folds of the fabric against her skin, thinking the dress fit extremely well considering that it hadn't been made for her. She adjusted the veil's netting about her shoulders and tilted her head first one way and then the other, wondering who had worn this dress before and who would wear it in the future.

It wouldn't be her, of course. Contrary to her attack of brilliance, she knew that West Ridgeman would never go down on his knees for any woman in a dress like this one. She could well imagine his reaction if he ever saw her in it. *Lovely dress,* he'd say as he favored her with his trademark smile, half-amused, half-serious. *A little underpowered for you, Sara, but lovely.*

Not that he or anyone else was going to see her wearing it, of course. She was taking it off right now, before her imagination fired off any more nutty ideas. Reaching for the back buttons, she caught a glint—a twinkle—in the mirror and turned to look at her reflection again. She had never had any patience for the fable of one man, one woman, one destiny. But something about this wedding dress made her think she might be wrong, made her wonder if perhaps there was a man meant especially for her, a love fated beyond her ability to command it.

With that thought, a man's reflection appeared in the mirror, and her heart broad jumped into her throat. She processed only the vaguest impressions— a gambler's stance, a loner's stare, a rogue's grin— before she spun to face him, her fists raised, ready to fight—and was embarrassed to find she was completely alone. Another glance in the mirror confirmed a solitary image—hers—and she exhaled slowly. There must have been something wrong with those fresh mushrooms she'd eaten at lunch. She'd call the grocery and complain. On second thought, she just wouldn't buy any more. Explaining that she was seeing *twinkles* was not likely to...

The back door opened with a familiar squeak and Sara froze. Maybe it hadn't been a hallucination. Maybe she had seen a man's reflection in the—

"Sara? Are you home?"

Her neighbor's voice was a mixed blessing. She felt instant relief that she wasn't about to face an intruder, but sincerely wished she wasn't about to face Gypsy, either. "I'm in the bedroom," she called, embarrassed to be caught clothed in her foolishness.

"I came over to see if you have any..." Gypsy's voice trailed off as she stopped short in the bedroom doorway. "Sorry, I must be in the wrong house. Unless..." She squinted, then waggled a finger. "Wait a minute. I recognize that frown. This is the right house and you are my neighbor, even if you are dressed funny."

"There's something funny about this dress, all right, but I am not laughing."

"Hmm. Curiouser and curiouser." Gypsy took a step closer. "Where did you get it?"

"Don't ask." Sara took off the veil and tossed it onto the bed. "It's a long story and I'm not proud of it. If you'll just help me get out of this dress, I'll be your friend forever."

"You'll be my friend forever, anyway. I want to hear the story. Every sordid word." Gypsy stepped over the bridal train and into the reflection in the dresser mirror. Her tummy protruded like a beach ball tucked under the picnic checks of her maternity blouse. "Confession is good for the soul, so spill your guts."

"It's embarrassing."

"All the better. Start at the very beginning and don't stop until I know every humiliating detail."

Sara shook her head at their Mutt and Jeff reflections, Gypsy, short and round with pregnancy, with her Kewpie doll haircut and her cheerleader smile, next to Sara, tall and sleek, with her auburn feather cut and unrevealing mouth. "Jason was supposed to pick up Alicia Randolph's wedding gown from the dry cleaners. This is what he brought home, instead."

"For a nineteen-year-old male, that was probably an honest mistake."

"Considering the cute and curvy seventeen-year-old female who works there during the summers, it probably was. However, if either one of them had paid the slightest attention, it would not have happened."

"It might have. You can't blame Jason for being young and irresistible to the opposite sex. It's the law of the jungle."

"Which somehow translates into a problem for me."

"Well, you can't tell me Jason made you put on this dress."

Embarrassing, but true. "No, that was the Gunnerson law of stupidity and I have to take full responsibility for it. I also have to get out of this dress. The owner of Starz called a little while ago. Apparently, someone came in to pick up this dress shortly after Jason left, and the mistake was discovered. They are sending someone to get this gown. They offered to drop off Alicia's dress at the same time, but I told them I'd pick it up in the morning. No sense in taking the chance of another mix-up."

"I guess Jason won't be making any more deliveries for At Your Service. At least, not for a while."

"He may have quit, for all I know. He was pretty angry when he left. I chewed him out for not being more responsible."

"You're awfully hard on him, Sara. He's just a kid."

"When I was his age, I worked two part-time jobs and carried seventeen hours a semester."

"Yes, and when you die, he will have that engraved on your tombstone. Give him a break. Just because he isn't as responsible or ambitious as you—"

"Period. He isn't ambitious, period." Sara took a deep breath, placed her hands on her waist and turned so that Gypsy could reach the back buttons. "I can't afford to worry about my brother tonight. I've got to be at West's house by six. You know how important tonight is for me. What time is it, anyway?"

"About five, I think." Gypsy tugged on the bodice. "Gee, these are tiny buttons. Now, tell me how you ended up in this dress and who buttoned you into it?"

Sara frowned in the mirror. "I buttoned it," she said. "It was easy."

"Right. Okay, we'll come back to that. What made you decide to put it on in the first place? Don't get me wrong, you look beautiful in the gown, but normally you wouldn't look twice at anything so... romantic."

"I don't understand it, either. Jason carried it into the house and something happened to me. It was like I was hypnotized or something."

"You?"

"I know it sounds unlikely, but I can't explain it any other way. The dress twinkled at me and the next thing I knew, I was wearing it."

Gypsy's eyes met hers in the mirror. *"Twinkled?"*

"All right, so I imagined that part. Maybe I even imagined that I put on the wedding gown."

"Nope. You're in it and I'm having a heck of a time trying to get you out of it. These are the tiniest button loops I have ever seen. Now, go back and start where the dress twinkled at you."

"Forget I said that."

"Not a chance. You are the least fanciful person I know, and if you say you were hypnotized by a dress, then I believe you."

"Well, I don't believe it. I cannot believe I am actually wearing this dress, either. Of all days to go completely insane..."

"Obviously, it's a sign. You're not supposed to marry West Ridgeman."

"Don't start that, Gyps," Sara warned. "Besides, he hasn't asked me, yet."

"Then there's still time to meet someone else, fall insanely in love and live happily ever after."

Laughter percolated in her throat. "That's about as likely as Kevin agreeing to any of the names you've picked out for the baby."

Gypsy stopped fumbling with the buttons. "It could happen."

"He's too sensible to call his child Sprite, and I'm too sensible to fall insanely in love with any man. Besides, West is everything I want in a husband. He's almost as ambitious as I am. He graduated from Harvard. He's successful, well-established in his career, well-respected—"

"Well-invested, well-insured and well-funded. I know this routine by heart."

Sara's defenses went into overdrive. "You know how mad I get when you say that. And you know it isn't true. Refusing to go out with men who are no match for me in drive and ambition does not make me mercenary. And I fail to see how refusing to go out with West because he is financially secure could make me a better person."

"You're right. However, you could, in good conscience, refuse to go out with him because he's boring and shallow."

"He is not. You don't know him like I do, Gyps. He's extremely intelligent and that sometimes makes people uncomfortable, but—"

"Enough already." Gypsy surrendered with both hands in the air. "I'm going for a Popsicle. Want one?"

"Can't you wait until after you get the buttons undone?"

"If I could control these cravings, Kevin wouldn't have bought two freezers and a twenty-four-foot meat locker. Besides, I'm not making any headway with these buttons, anyway. You may have to wear the wedding gown to the reception." She waddled to the doorway and down the hall, talking all the way. "Maybe West will be overcome with passion and propose on the spot."

Sara was startled to hear her own harebrained idea repeated aloud. It seemed an odd coincidence. On the other hand, everything seemed odd at the moment. "How am I supposed to get out of this dress?" she called.

"I'm just going to the kitchen. I know I'm not exactly Speedy Gonzalez, but I'll be back before you turn into an old maid."

Pressing her lips together in determination, Sara reached for the buttons at the back of the dress. She was going to get out of this ivory nightmare one way or another. The phone rang, spurring her motivation to get out of the bridal gown and into her own clothes. "Answer that, will you, Gyps?" she yelled down the hall.

"Got it," Gypsy yelled, and the phone stopped short on another ring.

The button loops proved obstinately tight, so Sara turned her attention to the sleeves. But even there, where she could coordinate her eye-hand movements, she met with no success. The buttons and loops would not come apart. Frustration rose and quickly doubled, hampering her efforts even more. Tonight's party was important to her, both personally and professionally. She didn't have time to fritter away trying to get out of a dress she should never have gotten into in the first place. Hypnotized by a wedding gown. That had to be the most ridiculous thought ever to sprout in her excessively practical brain.

She took a deep breath and renewed her attack on the buttons. In less than an hour, she would be with West. And she would not be wearing this dress, either. Bending down, she retrieved the black silk dress she had so carelessly discarded and laid it carefully on the bed. It had cost a king's ransom and could never be described as underpowered. She had bought it with West in mind—although she hadn't met him at the time—and it had been hanging at the back of her closet for over a year. But tonight was the debut. And if ever there was a dress to evoke a proposal of marriage...

"You haven't made much headway." Gypsy appeared in the doorway, a red Popsicle in her hand, her lips stained berry bright.

"I can't understand this. It was so easy to get into." The button battle took on the status of a personal grudge, and getting out of the dress became tantamount, somehow, to being the master of her own fate. "Who was on the phone?"

"Somebody Jackson." Gypsy licked a drip from the bottom of the Popsicle. "He has the Bubonic plague or something."

Sara swung her attention to Gypsy. "Not Sonny Jackson."

"Well, it's probably not the plague, but it's something contagious and—"

"He cannot do this to me. Not at five o'clock before a seven-thirty reception. Not *this* reception."

"Don't take it so personally. I'm sure he isn't any happier about it than you are. It's no fun to be contagious, you know."

"He isn't sick, Gypsy. He's a man who has no better ambition than to amuse himself and who will never be anything other than a mediocre, middle-class bartender. He's easily distracted and totally undisciplined. And this is the last time I'll hire him for any kind of job."

Gypsy pulled the Popsicle out of her mouth with a soft, slurpy pop. "He sounded sick."

"I don't doubt it, but I don't buy it, either. I'll call someone else."

"Who are you going to get this late?"

"I don't know. Someone. The worst-case scenario is that I'll have to tend bar myself." She was already reviewing a mental list of possible replacements, already moving toward the door and the employee files in the next room. "And I'm quite capable of doing that, if I have to."

"You're capable of single-handedly catering the whole affair while whistling 'Yankee Doodle' through your nose, but that doesn't mean—"

Sara barely listened as she passed Gypsy in the doorway and was only vaguely aware of the cumbersome satin brushing against the gingham checks. Panic made a roller-coaster loop through her stomach, but she shut it down with steady resolve. She would get out of this dress. Somebody on her list would be available to tend the bar. Somehow the evening would turn out exactly as she had planned.

A siren wailed in the distance as she entered the bedroom she used as an office. She moved to the desk, sharing her concentration between her two immediate problems. Lifting the phone receiver with one hand, she opened a notebook with the other and glanced at Gypsy, who had followed her as far as the doorway. "Could you try to unbutton the back of this dress while I make these calls?"

Gypsy pulled the remaining Popsicle from the stick with her teeth, then held up her berry-red fingertips. "I'll have to wash my hands," she said around a mouthful of red ice. "Be right back."

Sara nodded and resisted the urge to say, "Hurry." As she punched numbers on the dial pad, Gypsy waddled off down the hall, and a moment later the sound of running water came from the kitchen. On the other end of the phone line, there was the telltale click of an answering machine. Sara hung up and dialed the next number. Two busy signals and another answering machine later, the panic made a queasy return trip through her stomach. She punched in another set of numbers and waited. There had to be someone out there who needed a job, someone who would come through for her....

The sirens were louder suddenly, and the blare of a horn indicated an emergency vehicle approaching an intersection. Holding the phone to her ear, Sara bent down and looked out the window. The residential street looked as serene as a postcard, but the siren came closer and a fire truck rumbled into view and sped around the corner. A moment later, the siren stopped ... just in time for Sara to hear Gypsy's voice rise with panic.

"The chicken's on fire! The chicken's on fire!" The frantic announcement was followed almost instantaneously by the frantic slam of the kitchen door. Sara dropped the phone receiver and ran to the bathroom. She looked out the window and across the backyard just as a fireman carried a flaming pan outside and extinguished the blaze. Gypsy approached the fireman in an awkward, rolling walk, her arms waving with explanation, her head bobbing up to look at the fireman then down to look at the charred chicken.

Gypsy had burned Kevin's dinner... again. Sara moved away from the window and, in the stillness, heard a faint buzz. Realizing the phone was off the hook, she hurried to the office and picked up the dangling receiver. Whoever she'd called had hung up. With a muttered, "Damn," she punched redial and waited as the phone rang and rang. Just as she was about to try the next name on the list, a muted voice answered her call.

"Oh, uh...Clint," she said, finding the corresponding name and number in the notebook. "Sara Gunnerson from At Your Service. I have a job for you. Tonight. No, but it pays... I understand. Yes. Certainly. No problem. Next time, then." Slamming down the receiver provided not an ounce of satisfaction, and Sara twisted her arm behind her in another frustrating attempt to reach the annoyingly tiny buttons on the back bodice of the wedding dress. Glancing absently at the clock on her desk, she scanned the employee list again, hoping to see an overlooked name and num—

Five fifty-five.

With a belated surge of panic, her gaze swept to the clock. It couldn't be that late. Gypsy had said it was only five o'clock. But the second hand ticked steadily around the face, pushing the time closer and closer to six. Sara gave up all hope of finding a replacement for Sonny Jackson. There was no time for anything except getting out of this dress and into the other one.

She ran to her bedroom and jerked open drawers, looking for any sharp-edged instrument that might slit through the fabric loops and free her. She'd have to pay for the dress, of course, but how expensive could it be? And right now, she'd sell her birthright—if she had one—just to get out of the bridal gown and regain control of her life.

Plans skimmed through her mind like rocks skipping across a pond, each one quickly sinking to the bottom. She could call Gypsy and beg her to come back, but she hadn't been much help even before the chicken caught fire. She knew Jason wouldn't return her page, even if he had remembered to take the pager with him when he stormed out.

Her hand closed on a pair of scissors, and she withdrew them triumphantly from the drawer. And from the corner of her eye, she caught a glint in the mirror, a sparkle, a familiar *twinkle*.

She almost—almost—turned to look at her reflection, but she fought the impulse, refused to give in to it. That imaginary *twinkle* is what had gotten her into trouble in the first place and, even if it had been her imagination, she wasn't taking any more chances. She had assured West she'd be there. Tonight held the promise of all her tomorrows...and whimsy had no place in them.

However, it couldn't hurt to stay away from the mirror.

Turning her back on temptation, she grappled with the scissors, realizing abruptly that they were as dull as a butter knife and that even if they weren't, she couldn't see to cut the buttons off without looking in the mirror.

"All right," she muttered as she dropped the scissors into the drawer. She was going to West's party, and she was leaving now. She'd drive around the block to Gypsy's house and get her to unbutton the dress. With any luck, the fire department would still be there dousing the final embers of flaming chicken, and if worse came to worst, maybe they could use that jaws-of-death thing to get her out of the dress.

It wasn't a great plan, but it was the only one she could think of.

Slipping into her patent leather heels, she scooped up the black dress with one hand and her briefcase with the other and ran, as fast as the heavy satin skirt would allow, down the hall to the living room. Gathering up the skirt to keep it from dragging, she reached for the knob, jerked open the door and ran straight into a stranger's arms.

Chapter Two

Ben Northcross compared the numbers painted on the curb to the address written on the back of the Starz Laundry receipt. He'd expected an office building of one kind or another, and this dignified residential neighborhood was a surprise. The scatterbrained clerk at the dry cleaners had probably given him the wrong address. Considering that same clerk had erroneously handed over a million-dollar wedding dress to some pickup and delivery service, Ben figured the odds were better than even that whoever lived in this well-tended, modest home had never heard of the Starz Laundry and Dry Cleaners, much less of a company called At Your Service.

He positioned the kickstand, swung off the Harley with a single, practiced move and eyed the black Labrador retriever who sat, queenlike, in the sidecar. "Somewhere in this neighborhood is a kid who needs a dog, Cleo. I can just feel it. This is your chance to find a new home."

She looked at him, as she always did, with complete disdain and stayed where she was. He palmed his key ring, tossed it lightly in the air before catching it and slipping it into his pocket. "Suit yourself. You're going to have to share the sidecar with a wedding dress for the rest of the trip, but if it makes no difference to you, it certainly won't bother me."

Rising gracefully, the Lab hopped out of the sidecar and shook herself from nose to tail, conveying with unspoken eloquence that she would do exactly as she pleased. They had been together now for a little more than a year and she had yet to do anything he asked...like run away from home or pretend she liked him when he had company. Whoever had declared dogs to be man's best friend hadn't met Cleo. Her tolerance for him was only slightly less than his for her, but they were stuck with each other, and both of them knew it.

Placing his helmet on the seat, Ben looked at the house again, almost certain this would prove to be a wasted trip. He should have let the dry cleaners retrieve the dress and deliver it to him while he relaxed at some posh hotel. But the clerk had been so flustered, he had thought it would be quicker and easier just to get it himself. He walked around the motorcycle, stepped over the curb and onto the sidewalk.

Cleo trailed him indifferently as he approached the wide front porch, but he ignored her and wished with every step that he had never agreed to Pop's request to detour through Kansas City and fetch the wedding gown. Heaven knew, his sister Gentry had begged him not to. But Ben had learned by experience to avoid the middle of any battleground occupied by his tempestuous sister and their muleheaded father. He'd deliver the dress and let the two of them slug it out from there. At least, he would if he was at the right address. On second thought, maybe he ought to hope this was the wrong address.

He mounted the front steps and admired the wide and welcoming veranda. The porch swing beckoned, and he tried to imagine himself sitting there with a cold drink in his hand and a domestic goddess by his side as they watched their children play in the yard while dusk settled over the complacent and quiet neighborhood. If Cleo would lie at his feet, the whole scene could be captured in a Norman Rockwellesque painting. Which would probably be titled, *Someone's Wrong in This Picture*.

He raised his hand to knock, but before his knuckles made contact, the door burst inward and a bundle of redhead slammed into his arms. On most days, he would have caught her automatically and without having to give it a conscious thought. But he'd just ridden six straight hours on a motorcycle that had more promise than suspension. He'd spent four of the last five days jumping out of airplanes and parachuting into trees and rocky ravines. He was a mass of muscle aches, wired on too little sleep and too much overbrewed coffee, and the only automatic function he managed was to manipulate the fall to minimize injury. Consequently, he and the redhead hit the floor together and rolled, while her belongings scattered down the steps in a noisy clatter.

When he raised his head, he was on top of her, enjoying a moment or two of pleasant discovery before he acknowledged that she was in no mood to be appreciated. "Make my day," he said. "Tell me this is At Your Service."

Resignation echoed in her sigh. "I suppose you're from Starz Laundry and Dry Cleaners."

He grinned. "At your service and just in time to save you from breaking your neck."

"You got in my way."

"And stopped you from falling down the stairs."

"Should I be grateful that I'm being smothered by a delivery man instead?"

"Yes . . . and you're welcome."

Her russet eyes flashed with eloquent frustration. "You can jump to your feet any time, now."

"We fell pretty hard. It may take me a minute to recover." He liked the immediate and skeptical lift of her auburn brows. "Do you feel all right?"

Agitation simmered in her eyes. "Yes, and so do you. Now get off of me and don't give me any more nonsense about recovery time."

So she wasn't as naive as she looked . . . which was a pity. It seemed a shame to move, but Ben braced his weight on his hands, pushed up and levered to his feet. He stood for a second looking at the satin-bound bundle and admiring the auburn hair and fair-as-morning skin contrasted against the warm gray background of the porch. Leaning down, he offered his hand, but she got to her feet without any assistance and began slapping at the satin skirt like a cowgirl dusting off her chaps. A string of healthy, heartfelt epithets wisped past her lips, and Ben bit back a grin at the picture of aggravated motion before him. "Need some help?"

She didn't even look up. "I *need* a bartender and someone to get me out of this ridiculous dress."

The grin slipped past his control. "That sure beats the hell out of 'yes, please.' It just so happens that I possess the remarkable talent of opening beer bottles with my bare hands. And also, quite by chance, I have some small amount of experience in getting women out of ridiculous dresses."

She did look up then, her expressive eyes skimming across the scuffed toes of his boots, past his faded camouflage green dungarees, black T-shirt and tattered camouflage vest, and lingering on the dark, two-day stubble covering his chin. She said more in a glance than most women could say in five minutes, and it was quite clear that he wasn't going to get anywhere near her buttons.

"I have a sister," he offered as a reference. "She thinks I'm a reasonably nice guy."

Her gaze flicked to his. "I have a brother. He thinks I'm unreasonable and difficult."

"Are you?"

"Of course not. Look, I'm in something of a hurry right now. You'll have to excuse me." She turned and closed the door of the house, then hiked her skirt and flowed down the steps in a wash of ivory satin, pausing only long enough to gather her scattered belongings on the way. Ben watched with frank admiration of her graceful movements and with pleasurable appreciation for the pretty contrast of her dark red hair against the cream-colored lace. As she reached the bottom step, he registered belatedly that he was there to get a wedding gown and that she was wearing one. "Wait a minute. Is that your dress?" he asked.

She leaned down to scoop up a pool of black silk from the bottom step. "Only if you're of the opinion that possession is nine-tenths of the law."

He frowned. "So it's *not* your dress?"

"No. It's the dress you were sent to pick up."

"No one mentioned that it came prepackaged and complete with the bride."

"It doesn't and I'm not." She pursed her eloquent lips in an impatient frown. "Look, I can't take the time to explain it right now. I have a very important date."

"Shotgun wedding?" he suggested.

"Not even close. I'm sorry, but I'm very late and this reception is very important. You can wait if you want or come back later." The satin skirt swished in tempo with her rush down the remaining steps. At the bottom, she bent down and reached for the briefcase, which had opened in the tumble down the stairs and now formed an inverted vee of expensive leather.

"You're not going to give me the dress?" he asked, just to be sure he understood.

She pitched things into the briefcase with a controlled intensity. "Nothing would provide me more pleasure than to hand it over right now. However, that isn't possible, so if you'll leave your name and address, I'll be happy to rush over with the gown first thing in the morning."

"What if I can't wait that long?"

"Starz has already closed for the evening," she said knowledgeably. "What are you going to do with the dress tonight, anyway?"

"I believe the question is, what are *you* going to do with it?"

Picking up the briefcase, she took a step down the front walk. "I am going to get out of it, one way or another. Then I'm going to hang it in the back of the van and cover it with a blanket or something dark so I can't see it. Now, you can follow along if you want to keep an eye on this bewitching outfit, but believe me, I have no designs on this dress except to see it safely in your hands."

"So why are you wearing it?"

"It's a long story and I don't have time to go into it."

"You may have more time than you think. I don't believe you're going anywhere right away."

She looked at him, the expression in her eyes blending surprise and temper. "If you're attempting to threaten me, I think you should know that I've been taking care of myself longer than you've owned that guerrilla warfare vest, and I'm not frightened by punks like you."

"Punk?"

"All right, so you're a little long in the tooth to be a punk. But if the attitude fits..."

"It isn't my attitude you should worry about. It's hers." He leveled a finger and Cleo barked in response.

The woman jerked back, clearly startled. "Where did that come from?"

"She rode in on the Harley. I wouldn't mess with her if I were you."

"Does she belong to you?"

"We just travel together."

"She's guarding my car keys."

"I know."

Impatience flashed in her russet eyes. "Well, tell her to get away from them."

"Stay, Cleo," he said sternly. "Don't move."

With an independent wag of her tail, Cleo stayed, front paws planted strategically on either side of the key chain that had tumbled from the briefcase into the grass.

Ben shrugged at the redhead's furious stare. "If I'd told her to move, a bulldozer couldn't have rooted her out. The best thing you can do is ignore her."

"What do you mean, ignore her? I have to have those keys. I'm already late." She stepped forward purposefully.

"Don't...." His protest dissolved into a low groan as Cleo grabbed the keys in her mouth and ran a fast figure eight across the lawn. "Now see what you've done."

"What *I've* done? It's *your* dog."

"Only in the most technical sense."

"Just tell her to drop the keys."

"You saw what happened when I told her to stay."

"Yes, she stayed."

He shook his head. "Only because she knew I really wanted her to move."

With short, angry motions, the redhead lifted her skirt and headed toward the dog. It was exactly the wrong thing to do, but she obviously had a mind of her own. She might even prove a match for Cleo. Ben crossed his arms and settled back to watch.

OF ALL TIMES for the world to go berserk, Sara thought as she approached the big black dog. Her hopes for the evening were fading fast. "Give me those keys," she demanded.

The dog took off like a rocket, circling the yard—and Sara—half a dozen times before crouching in the grass to wait for the next overture.

"Stay." She issued the command with authority and held her hand out like a policeman halting traffic. "Stay," she said again and took a cautious step toward the dog...who lay motionless. Another step and Cleo wagged her tail. Another and she was off like a shot, racing around the yard again, keys dangling from her mouth, a picture of canine delight.

Sara frowned at the man on her porch. "Don't you have any control over her?"

"None," he admitted with irritating good nature. "But you're not doing so badly. At least she's staying in the yard."

"She isn't going to disappear with my keys, is she?"

"I doubt it. She likes to keep an eye on me."

Despite her current state of agitation, Sara could understand that, at least. He had a roguish look about him, and the loose-fitting clothes he wore did little to disguise the muscular body he seemed so comfortable in. As if she had time to notice such trivia. "Are you just going to stand there and do nothing about your dog?"

He had a scoundrel's smile. "Having both of us chase her around the yard will only make matters worse. I've played this game before, and the best thing you can do is to ignore her."

Sara closed her eyes tight and wished to start the day all over. And this time, she wouldn't touch the wedding dress. And she'd leave early for the reception and avoid this man and his dog from the outset. "This could ruin my life," she said, thinking aloud. "Is she susceptible to bribes?"

He shrugged. "She'll do almost anything for a Fig Newton."

"What about a Popsicle? Would she go for that?"

"Probably."

Her spirits lifted with the possibility that maybe the evening wasn't ruined, maybe there was still a chance to get the keys and... "I shut the door," she said with a heavy sigh. "It locks automatically and the—"

"Key is on the keychain." He finished the sentence for her and trotted down the steps to stand beside her. "Is that your van parked across the street? The one with A Vice painted on the side panel?"

"That's it," she said, feeling worse by the minute. "Those flowery letters cost a fortune, and two weeks ago, they spelled At Your Service. Of course, that was before my brother came to work for me."

"Look on the bright side. It isn't everyone who can advertise their business as A Vice, and you can't tell me that isn't an attention-getter. Is it locked?"

"I doubt it. Why? Can you hot-wire it?"

"I was thinking more along the lines of coaxing Cleo inside. She likes to travel, and even if she doesn't drop the keys, it shouldn't be hard to get them away from her once she's in."

"It's worth a try, I guess." Sara set off across the street, grumbling silently about people who treated their animals like humans and didn't teach them the first thing about obedience. She opened the back doors of the van, set her briefcase inside and draped the black dress across it. Turning, she clapped her hands. "Come on, Cleo. Come on, girl. Want to go for a ride? Let's go. Come on."

The keys jangled as the Lab loped across the street and jumped into the van. Sara slammed the doors, not sure exactly what she had just accomplished.

"The keys are in the van," she said. "Now what?"

He crossed the street to join her. "You're set. She's ready to go."

Sara moved around the van until she could see Cleo sitting in the passenger seat, ready to ride. "I guess this means she's going with me."

"Unless you'd rather leave her here and take my Harley."

The dismal appearance of the motorcycle parked in front of her house didn't inspire confidence, and she shook her head. "No, thanks. I'll take my chances with Cleo." Sara started around the front of the van, then paused. "She's not going to expect to drive, is she?"

"No, but she will want to attend the reception. She's very sociable."

"I don't suppose she can mix drinks."

"Not unless you count Gravy Train." He paused. "You know, of the two of us, I'd be more help to you than Cleo will. She's not going to be of much assistance in getting you out of that dress."

True statement. And Sara did not want West to catch even a glimpse of her looking like the queen of hearts. "Have you ever done any bartending?"

"You're looking at the unofficial champion of the 1983 Daytona Beach Beer Before Liquor contest," he said modestly.

"I hope that means you know the difference between a beer and a bourbon."

"I can also distinguish between a domestic and an imported beer."

"So can I...as long as no one takes off the labels." She weighed her level of desperation against his rough-and-tumble appearance. "Do you have anything else to wear? A tuxedo, maybe?"

He snapped his fingers. "I knew I shouldn't have left my tux in the other knapsack."

"Sorry. Just thinking aloud." She assessed him for another couple of seconds, then came to a decision and thrust out her hand. "I'm Sara Gunnerson, the owner of At Your Service."

"Ben Northcross." He engulfed her hand in a forceful clasp that lingered a heartbeat too long.

She resisted the impulse to curl her fingers over the warmth in her palm. "Do you have to take the dress back to the laundry tonight? Is someone waiting for you to deliver it somewhere else?"

"No and no."

"Good." She breathed a tiny sigh of relief. "Here's the deal. Whatever you're getting paid to pick up and deliver this dress for the dry cleaners, I'll double it. Hourly rate or flat fee. Maximum of a hundred dollars for the night. The contract ends at midnight, and you pocket any tips. Is that okay with you?"

"Sounds fair."

"Great. Let's go." Moving briskly, she walked around the van to the driver's side. "You'll have to get in on this side. That door won't open."

He approached her as she stood in the angle of the open door. "What happened?"

"My brother, Jason, was on his way to deliver pizzas to a Little League picnic and he pulled out in front of a truck with tires big enough to crush a small town. Fortunately, no one was injured, we only lost two of twelve pizzas, and the van still runs. Unfortunately, I can only afford liability insurance, so the side panel won't be undergoing cosmetic surgery for at least a few more months."

"Why was he delivering pizzas in your van?"

"That's what I pay him to do."

"Just exactly what is your business, Sara?"

For some reason, his use of her name unsettled her, but it was a little late to insist on formality. "At Your Service provides a potpourri of services. Whatever the job, I find someone to do it."

"Like hiring me to get you out of your dress?"

With a slight arch of her brows, she wondered if she'd made a mistake in hiring him on the spot as she had. His image, certainly, wasn't up to her standards. Although, when he smiled, his scruffy appearance took on a certain rough appeal. He was articulate and intelligent, both strong points in his favor. And she was desperate...which was the deciding factor. "More like hiring you to tend bar at a private party."

"Damn." His smile was sexy and slow. "I was hoping you had taken one look at me and fallen into instant lust."

She noted his seductive, green-eyed amusement and answered it with her own amiable, I'm-the-boss stare. "Sorry, Ben, but lust—instant or otherwise—is one thing I steer clear of, especially with employees."

His eyebrows lifted, as did the corners of his mouth. "No fringe benefits with this job, I take it."

"You catch on quick. I like that in a man. Get in the van and see if you can persuade your dog to move to the back and let you ride shotgun." She gave him extra room to move past her... and he still managed to brush against her, his arm stroking along her shoulder in a casually accidental touch, a touch calculated to warn her that he was temptation and she could be tempted. Which was good to know right from the start.

"The bartender I'd hired for tonight stood me up," she explained as Ben showed her a camouflaged but muscular backside before he slid behind the steering wheel. His biceps knotted beneath the sleeves of his faded black T-shirt as he grabbed Cleo's collar and urged her to hop in back. The struggle for a first-class seat was brief and decisive, leaving Cleo out of luck and looking offended in the back of the van while Ben levered across the console and settled into the passenger's seat. Sara noted the ease of his movements, along with his physique and probable strength, rating her response as merely an intriguing curiosity. "That's the worse part of this business," she continued as if her thoughts hadn't been on his impressive body, "having to depend on undependable people."

"So I look dependable to you?"

"You look available, and right now, that's more important to me." She grabbed the steering wheel in one hand, scooped up the satin skirt in the other and swung into the driver's seat. It took a moment to gather the skirt inside and another to tuck the ivory folds around her before she could shut the car door. Once settled, she reached for the ignition, then turned to Ben. "Your dog still has my car keys."

He turned in the seat and frowned at the Labrador. "Keys, Cleo," he said sternly. "We're not leaving until you hand them over."

The dog panted in reply, the keys nowhere in sight.

"I'll climb back there and look around. They must be here somewhere." Rising in the seat, Ben put one leg over the console and looked at Sara. "And I know what you're thinking."

"That obedience training should be mandatory for dogs and their owners?"

"No. You're thinking, I'd better get my butt in gear because we're really late." He squeezed between the seat belts. "I probably should have told you I also have an amazing ability to read minds."

He was right about one thing, she *had* been thinking about his butt. "Too bad you can't read Cleo's. Her thoughts would be far more instructive than mine."

"Nah, she'd lead us on a wild-goose chase—make that wild-key chase—at the first opportunity. No sign of your key ring back here." He moved aside a cardboard box. "Just a box marked Randolph Reception."

"Perfect," Sara said glumly. "We have everything we need to coordinate tomorrow's wedding, and not one single thing for tonight's party."

"You have a bartender," Ben pointed out.

"Who has no clothes."

"I beg your pardon. I'm fully dressed."

"You can't tend bar looking like that."

He stepped around Cleo and moved to the front of the van. "What's wrong with the way I look? My mother always told me I was handsome."

"Well, my father told me that clothes make the man. As soon as we get there, I'm going to find something else for you to wear."

"That should be interesting. I can see you now. Measuring guests as they enter, asking them if they'd mind terribly changing clothes with me."

She sighed, frustrated by the delay. "Do you see the keys anywhere?" Her gaze fell on the passenger seat. "Oh, wait. You were sitting on them. Cleo must have dropped the ring in your seat before you got in."

"Always thinking of me, aren't you, Cleo?"

The dog thumped her tail once, then began sniffing her way around the van, exploring her new surroundings. Sara inserted the key into the ignition and started the motor. "I cannot believe I'm going to be late. I'm never late. Not even for dental appointments. What time is it? No, don't tell me. I'd rather not know." She gunned the engine, checked the side mirror, then pulled away from the curb with a squeal of tires.

Ben dropped into his seat and buckled his seat belt with a decisive snap. "Where are we going?"

Just being on the move made Sara feel more encouraged. "The West Ridgeman house."

"What is that? A nursing home?"

"It's a private residence owned by West Ridgeman."

"And he is?"

"The man I'm going to marry."

The quick turn of his head toward her marked his surprise. "Is that why you're wearing the wedding dress?"

Her rising spirits took a nosedive. "No. The last thing I want is for West to see me in this."

"Oh, right. It's supposed to be bad luck or something."

Sara took her eyes off the road long enough to frown at him. "I would never wear anything this old-fashioned or this traditional when I get married. West would hate it. Besides, he doesn't know he's going to marry me."

"He doesn't?"

"Not yet."

"When are you planning to tell him?"

"I'm not. He'll come up with the idea all on his own, and I'll be overcome with blushing surprise."

"Hmm. I didn't know it worked that way. Of course, I've never been married, but I always assumed it would be something of a mutual decision."

"Someone has to plan these things," she said. "West is perfect for me. I knew it the first moment I set eyes on him. I've just had to nudge him around to my way of thinking."

"So he's about to be blindsided by love at first sight." Ben rubbed his chin. "What a concept."

"It isn't new. It isn't even original. Men and women have been doing it for centuries."

"Really? Does Mother Nature know about this?"

Sara turned her head to look at him, noting the threadbare sheen of his camouflage pants, liking the wise-guy glint in his eyes despite her better judgment. "Who do you think invented it in the first place? But there are always people like you who think there's something fundamentally wrong with giving a prospective relationship a push in the right direction."

"What if it turns out to be the wrong direction?"

"Check for traffic on your side. The side mirror was knocked out of whack in the accident."

Ben looked over his shoulder at the lane of highway on the right. "You're clear after the red car."

"Thanks."

"No problem. It's the least I can do in exchange for this fascinating lesson on male-female bonding."

"Make fun of the idea if you want, but it happens all the time."

"I believe you. I just prefer to stick with the idea that falling in love is something that can't be planned. It just happens."

"Right. And somewhere out there in your future is a woman who will plot every step of your walk down the aisle to happily ever after. All the experts agree that good marriages require work, but no one talks about working at the relationship before marriage."

"You've obviously given this a lot of thought, but I'll stick to my theory of the lightning bolt. Your way sounds too labor intensive."

"I waited a long time to meet the right man and he's worth the effort."

"So how did you find this paragon?"

"Through my business. At Your Service provides services for events like West's party tonight. I'm supplying a bartender and two servers, a husband-and-wife team, who I hope are already there and ready to go. West contracted for my services, just as I contracted for yours. It's a mutually beneficial relationship."

"So after you're married, who's going to wash the dishes?"

She looked at him, then honked the horn as the van came up behind a slow-moving station wagon in the left, keep-it-moving, lane of traffic. "We'll hire someone."

"I see." Ben tightened his seat belt. "That still doesn't explain why you're wearing the wedding dress."

"It was a mistake."

"That you got in it? Or that you couldn't get out of it?"

The station wagon changed lanes, and Sara floored the accelerator. "I'm going to plead the Fifth."

"You're going to be pleading in traffic court, if you don't slow down."

"I'm not going that fast."

"The defense will have to call me as a hostile witness, then."

"Relax." She leaned close to him, trying to check traffic in the crooked right-hand mirror. "Am I clear?" At his nod, she changed lanes. "Think of all the money you'll make tonight. More than you've seen in quite a while."

"What makes you think that?" His voice was resonant with offended dignity, and she wished she hadn't mentioned his circumstances. Men were always so touchy about money...or rather about a woman *knowing* they didn't have any.

"I've done my share of delivery work. I know what a pittance it pays."

"Maybe this is a special delivery."

She gave him a conciliatory smile. "Look, Ben, it doesn't matter to me if you're a little down on your luck. It's nothing to be ashamed of. I know. I've been there myself. To be honest, I've been there so many times it feels like home. But tonight is going to be a turning point for me. I'm moving up in the world. Maybe some doors will open up for you, too." She glanced at him. "Providing we can get you out of those clothes."

"I thought I was supposed to get you out of your clothes."

"Dress," she corrected quickly. "Dress only."

"Hope springs eternal."

"Below a man's waistline, at any rate."

His gaze fastened on her again, and then slowly, almost reluctantly, he smiled. "You are a piece of work, Ms. At Your Service."

"Thank you."

"There's a car pulling into your lane ahead. You might want to slow down."

Her foot didn't budge off the accelerator. "I'm an excellent driver," she said. "And I'm very good at what I do."

"I don't doubt it. I just wish you'd do it slower."

"Obviously, you're not a risk taker. I'm in complete control. There is nothing to worry about."

"What about him?"

"Who?"

"The policeman on your tail."

She glanced at the mirror and caught the unmistakable flash of yet another delay. "He's trying to get around me, that's all. I'll just change lanes and get out of the way."

"I've noticed that risk takers are generally optimists."

Behind her, the red lights continued to flash their warning, and Sara tightened her grip on her temper as she pulled to the shoulder. "Would you mind getting my driver's license from my briefcase? It's in the back."

"Sure." Ben unbuckled the belt and climbed over the seats again. "Move over, Cleo. And you may as well stop pouting. It doesn't become you and you're not getting the front seat."

Cleo grumbled, stood up and shook herself.

Sara frowned fiercely at the police car reflected in the side mirror. "Come on," she said impatiently to the patrolman who had, as yet, not opened his door. "I'm in a hurry. I don't know why it takes them so long to get out of their cars. This is why people hate getting stopped for traffic violations. It takes so damned long to get the ticket."

Ben dropped the license in her lap. "You're right," he agreed. "It's harassment, pure and simple."

She looked up with a frown, which he met with an easy grin. Feeling foolish, she turned her frustration where it belonged. "If this stupid dress hadn't twinkled at me, none of this would have happened."

He dropped into the seat beside her. "Did you say *twinkled?*"

"Yes, and don't ask." Thumping the steering wheel with her hand, she checked the mirror for advancing traffic cops. "Come on," she muttered, then tapped her fingers impatiently on the console. "If there is anything else that can go wrong this evening, I don't know what it could be."

"I don't know, either," Ben said. "But I'm beginning to think the possibilities are endless."

Chapter Three

Ben watched Sara roll down the window and prepare to face the inconsiderate policeman who had stopped her. She extended her license and vehicle registration in cool silence while her foot tapped impatiently against the floorboard. Before he'd stepped onto her porch, all Ben had had on his mind was a cold beer, a hot shower and a bed with clean sheets. Which only proved he'd set his expectations for the evening far too low.

He was rarely surprised, but she had rushed into his arms, knocked him off his feet and captured his curiosity with her first words to him. He'd been intrigued every moment since. In thirty-four years, he'd heard every come-on, seen every angle, gotten cornered by the best and lived to tell about it. But until today, he'd never had anyone size him up in a glance and conclude he'd do in a pinch. Sara was a new experience, and that was a novelty in itself. If Cleo hadn't grabbed those keys, Ben knew he would have figured out some other way to get invited along on this ride.

The patrolman stepped up to the open window, took the papers dripping from Sara's hand and studied them for several long moments, never once look-ing directly into the van. "Do you have any idea how fast you were driving, ma'am?"

"Seventy?"

The officer clicked his ballpoint pen and began copying information onto the citation. "I clocked you at eighty-three."

"Really? Hmm. I wasn't aware of going that fast. You see, I'm very late for a—"

"Nothing is important enough to risk your life, or the lives of others."

"I know, Officer, and I promise I'll drive the speed limit for the rest of my life."

"Sign here." The officer thrust the clipboard through the window, and Sara scrawled her name across the signature line.

"There." She handed it back and tapped her fin-gertips on the steering wheel until he returned a copy of the citation, along with her license and registra-tion. She jammed the papers under the sun visor, started the engine and smiled politely at the patrol-man. "Please step aside. We're a little behind sched-ule." With that, she put the van in gear and zoomed forward, honking as she merged into the flow of traf-fic.

Ben was impressed by her ability to stay focused. "Great exit line."

"It would have been better if it had come a little sooner."

"Any sooner or faster and you would have torn the ticket right out of the book for him."

"I'm in a hurry."

The sound of a siren came faint but insistent behind them. "I think he's aware of that."

Sara glanced in the mirror. "What does he want now?"

"Probably wants to tear up the speeding ticket and give you a medal for bravery."

With a frown, she pulled onto the shoulder again and stopped with a jerk. When the cruiser pulled in behind, her foot started tapping out her impatience once again. "I really don't have time for this."

"I don't think I'd tell him that."

She rolled down her window, and Ben settled back to observe round two.

"License and registration, please." The patrolman took his time in removing the pen from his pocket and clicking the ballpoint into place.

Sara gave a frustrated sigh as she jerked them from behind the visor and handed them over. "What did you clock me at that time?"

"I'm citing you for failure to yield to oncoming traffic and not heeding a legal warning to slow your speed."

"I was barely moving when I pulled out," she said in a huff, then took a deep breath and changed her tune. "I'm sorry. You're absolutely right. I will slow down and yield to traffic. And I won't honk the horn anymore, either." She held up her hand, palm out. "Scout's honor. Now can I go?"

"You can go just as soon as I finish writing out this ticket."

"Is it going to take long? I'm really late."

The patrolman slowly pulled off his sunglasses, withdrew a handkerchief from his pocket and carefully wiped the lens. "Where are you going in such a rush?" As he started to replace the glasses, he seemed to notice her clothing for the first time. "Are you on your way to be married?"

"I was before you stopped me, but I don't know now. You may have ruined my life in one—make that two—attempts to meet your daily quota of traffic tickets."

Ben rubbed his jaw, awed by her audacity, amazed that the patrolman appeared to swallow it with a smile, hook, line and sinker. He adopted a noncommittal expression when the officer pointed at him with a frown. "He doesn't look like a bridegroom."

"He doesn't look like a bartender, either," Sara said. "But that's what he is."

The policeman oriented himself with a glance at the highway signs, then addressed Ben. "Where are you going? The church on Mission Park Road?"

Ben shrugged. "I'm from out of town."

"There's a church on Mission Park Road," Sara confirmed.

The officer turned his attention to her. "Would that be the Methodist church?"

"Maybe." Sara's smile was all anxiety. "I'm not thinking too clearly at the moment."

The patrolman nodded his understanding. "Nervous, huh?"

"Getting more so by the second."

He looked at Ben. "What about you?"

"I'm nervous, too."

"The way she drives, you'd be a fool not to be. You may be getting a lot more than you bargained for."

"Yes," Ben said with a smile. "That thought has occurred to me."

The patrolman tore the ticket out and handed it to Sara. "You can tear that up. My wedding gift to you. But you've got to slow down. And the speeding ticket stands."

"Thank you, Officer," she said. "That's very kind, and I hope you'll understand when I say that the next time I'm in a hurry, I hope you're off duty."

She rolled up the window and put the car in gear, but she did wait until the patrolman had turned his back and was walking toward his vehicle before she peeled out. "Honestly, don't the police have better things to do? I mean, it isn't like I was shooting at motorists or anything."

"True."

"And I always use signal lights when I change lanes."

"I noticed."

"He should be out catching real criminals, not stopping law-abiding... What is he doing now?" She frowned at the mirror, then turned her head to look at Ben. "Can you believe it? He's going to pull me over again."

Ben bent to look in the side mirror. "I think he's going to escort us to the church on Mission Park Road."

"Why would he do that?"

"Probably because you told him you were getting married there and that you were late."

"I didn't tell him that. I said I was late, which is true. And I said I'm on my way to be married, which is true when you consider the overall scheme of my life. I'm just not on my way to be married tonight."

"You should have given him directions to the West Ridgeman house. Then he could have escorted you somewhere you actually want to go." Ben paused. "I'm not sure, but I think I saw the dress twinkle at him."

"That isn't funny," she snapped.

The patrol car pulled around them in a flash of lights and the siren came on with an intrusive congratulations. Ben crossed his arms and settled back in the seat. "I love the VIP treatment."

"Don't get too comfortable with it. I'm going to lose him at the next exit ramp."

"Why would you want to do that?"

"Because I don't want to detour by the Methodist church."

"Are you always this spontaneous?"

"No." She switched lanes, following the speeding black and white. "I like to know exactly where I'm going and exactly how much time I need to get there. And until today, that has not been a problem."

"What happened today?" He couldn't resist humming a couple of bars of "Twinkle, Twinkle, Little Star."

"Would you forget about that?" Her sidelong and unamused glance delighted him. "I only imagined that. It didn't really happen. And I am not going to slip and say it again."

"I thought it was charming."

"Uh-huh. Now, check for traffic on your side, because I'm taking the next exit."

"What about our escort?"

"With any luck, he won't look in his rearview mirror for the next mile or so."

"I doubt that reaching the church and discovering we're not behind him will make him happy."

"Another delay will not make me happy. So there you have it."

Ben looked over his right shoulder to check for cars in the inside lane. "You're clear."

She shot across both lanes of traffic and down the exit ramp, turning left on a yellow light, passing under the viaduct and taking the entrance ramp onto the expressway heading in the opposite direction. "We'll get off at the next exit, and by the time he realizes we're not behind him, we'll be out of sight."

"Have you considered stunt work as a career?"

She rolled her eyes. "What kind of idiot risks life and limb for the sake of someone else's entertainment?"

"Oh, I don't know. You're risking your life and limbs—and mine, too, incidentally—just to get to a party."

"It isn't just any party."

"I certainly hope not, considering the amount of frenetic energy you've invested in eluding the police, not to mention the monetary contribution you'll be making to the city coffers if that officer ever catches up with you."

"What's he going to do? Write another ticket? Even if he tracks me down, after tonight I'll be able to afford it."

"Really? Why? Is West going to announce your engagement and his intention of paying all your traffic tickets?"

"I told you, West doesn't know he's going to marry me. At least, he didn't the last time we were together. But he might make a special announcement tonight that could put my balance sheet over the top."

"And that is . . . ?"

"I can't tell you, but it's important."

"He's going to run for president and you're in charge of the coffers."

She shook her head. "Politics is not on his agenda. Or mine. Right now, the only thing I'm worried about is making the right impression on his friends and associates."

"Why would you worry about that?"

"Because my future depends on it. If I make a good impression, not only will I get new clients, affluent clients, but West will begin to see me as a part of his social group and less as strictly a business associate." She glanced at him. "I'm sure it sounds ridiculous to you, but for a girl who was born on the wrong side of the tracks, this is the light at the end of the tunnel. I'm not going to blow it."

Something in her voice and in the set of her chin told Ben more than he wanted to know about Sara Gunnerson, and some lingering trace of sensitivity in his calloused heart went out to her. "So this is a career milestone and a personal step up the social ladder."

"I wouldn't put it exactly like that. For me, being invited to attend this party as a guest means my plans are becoming reality. It marks the beginning of achieving the goals I've set for myself." The van sailed down the next exit ramp and made a left, merging into the Friday evening rush hour. "Providing, of course, that I can get out of this wedding gown before West sees me."

"The *twinkling* wedding gown." He teased her gently, hoping to see her smile.

To his surprise, she laughed instead. A throaty, heart-stopping, womanly amusement made all the more charming because she was laughing at herself. "A twinkling wedding gown. Isn't that the dumbest thing you've ever heard?"

"In the last hour? No, I think that would have to be when you said that dress wasn't your style. You must know you look enchanting in it."

Her glance was skeptical. "Flattery will get you only as far as the driver's seat."

"I get to drive the A Vice van?"

"Since this model didn't come equipped with autopilot, you'll have to take over while I change. Unless you want Cleo to drive."

"She has so many vices her license was suspended."

"Then that makes you the designated driver, providing that your license hasn't been suspended, too."

"I'm legal."

"Then I'm not making any great leap of faith, am I?"

"I'd say the leap of faith came when you offered me a job."

"Oh, that was a little unorthodox, maybe, but hardly any great risk. I wouldn't worry too much about tonight. West is quite a connoisseur of wine, and the most exotic drink you'll have to mix will probably be a gin and tonic." She leaned down and released a lever. The seat slid back as she scooted to the edge in order to keep her foot on the pedal. "Now, slip in behind me and take the steering wheel."

"Now?"

She frowned at him. "Yes, now."

"Wouldn't it be easier to pull over and stop the vehicle before trading places?"

"Are you always so careful? Don't answer that. It doesn't matter. I've already stopped twice, and I don't have time to do it again. My entire future hinges on what happens tonight, and I am not going to arrive any later than I already am." She wiggled closer to the edge of the seat. "Now, there's plenty of room, so just put your leg over, straddle the seat and ease your way down."

He looked through the windshield at the moderately heavy traffic. They were careening down a busy street like a duck doing the backstroke, and she wanted to switch drivers. He couldn't believe she thought stunt work posed any great risk. Maybe he ought to offer *her* a job. "You're the boss." He released the seat restraint, levered up and over, and in two moves and a quick slide, he was cupping her body in the curve of his... and thinking that in this instance, the reward definitely outweighed the risk. He enjoyed the feel of her nestled between his thighs and admired the warm ivory of her back contrasted against the pattern of ivory lace that covered it. Nerves of steel and skin like silk. Now that was an interesting combination.

"What are you waiting for?" Her voice vibrated with urgency. "Unbutton me."

"Shouldn't we kiss first?"

"In your wildest dreams." She wiggled her shoulders as if that alone would motivate him.

"You could be missing an earth-shattering experience."

"I'll live with the regret."

He touched his fingertip to the only uncovered swatch of creamy skin and stroked across it, wanting her to experience some discomfort, if not some second thoughts about picking up strangers. "What if I can't?" he said provocatively. "What if I don't want to?"

Her laugh evolved slowly, percolating in her throat before bubbling over and sending the husky notes streaming over him in a warm, pleasurable rush. "Aren't you the least bit leery of hitting on a woman in a wedding gown? This dress has commitment written all over it, and I'd bet the ranch that you're the kind of guy who starts singing, 'Don't Fence Me In' after the second date." She shook her head, and her hair brushed her shoulders in a silky, dark wave. "You don't scare me, Ben. I had you pegged long before I invited you to climb into this van with me. Now, be the nice guy you really are and unbutton the dress."

So much for teaching her a lesson. He dropped his hands to the buttons. "You're far too trusting, Sara. You might have pegged me wrong."

"But I didn't," she said with aggravating confidence. "I'm probably the least trusting person you will ever encounter, but I do trust my own judgment, and my intuition almost never steers me wrong."

"There's always a first time."

The glance she attempted to throw over her shoulder fell short, so she gave her hair a provocative toss.

"All right, I can see that you're not convinced, so try this on for size. You're honest and intelligent—that I can tell from your eyes. I can tell by your appearance you're down on your luck and by the set of your jaw that you're not desperate. I can tell by the way you look at me that you have a basic respect for women. And I can tell by your tone of voice that you expect to be respected, as well. The way you hold your shoulders tells me you have too much pride, and your not-quite-macho walk tells me you are confident and secure with your masculinity. I can tell by the touch of your hands that you're not accustomed to taking no for an answer, but there's a certain restraint that tells me you're not afraid to be gentle. How am I doing so far?"

"Did you get my bank balance, too? Or should I tear a few more holes in my vest?"

She honked at a slow-moving car in front of them and swung the van onto a side street. "Your bank balance is of no importance to me, Ben. I just need your body for a few hours. The rest is incidental."

He couldn't recall ever being dismissed so easily or with such blunt conceit. The fact that she did, in many ways, have him pegged was doubly irritating. "You're amazingly arrogant...even for a redhead."

"I hate that. Women don't refer to men as a hair color. I would never call you a blackhead."

"My hair isn't black." He couldn't quite keep the insult from echoing in his voice.

"Okay, so what color is your hair?"

"It's dark brown." He was beginning to wish he'd opted for the beer, bath and bed. "I'm surprised you couldn't tell that by the way I bend my knees."

Her laugh came again, another low, husky tremor in her throat. "I'm sorry if I offended your vanity, but you did ask for it."

He didn't believe he'd asked for any such thing. "Let me get this straight. If I refer to you as a redhead, I'm being sexist. But you can size me up in a matter of minutes based on my appearance, and you're just being intuitive?"

"That's right."

"Ah, I see. This is the old double standard at play."

"No. This is twenty-eight years of observation and experience at work. The old live-and-learn axiom."

"And you're never wrong."

"I didn't say that. I'm just not wrong about you." She was so sure of herself, so naively certain.

"How do you know?"

She lifted one shoulder in a delicate shrug. "There's no need to feel threatened. I'm not psychic. I can't read your mind."

Ben closed his eyes for a moment. She was incredible.

"This isn't some special gift. I had to look out for myself and my younger brother when I was growing up, and that meant learning how to size up the danger in situations and in people."

"And I pose no danger." He allowed his fingers to graze her skin and felt her quicksilver response.

"No," she said with a touch of bravado. "Although if you don't hurry, I could be in danger of arriving very overdressed for this reception."

"You can borrow my vest if you want. That would add a casual touch."

"I brought something else to wear. Something much more suitable for this evening and far more becoming."

"That's hard to imagine." Ben worked at the tiny buttons, opening an ever-widening V of smooth, soft skin. "Frankly, I think you're missing a golden opportunity with West by not making certain he gets to see you in this. He could start hearing wedding bells after just one twinkle."

Her shoulders stiffened suddenly, as if a hidden straight pin had jabbed her. "He would think it was a practical joke . . . and not a good one, either."

"Why do you say that?"

"I know his tastes, and he would never want his bride to wear anything so unfashionable." Her hips moved within the curvature of his thighs as she applied the brakes, then again when she accelerated, and his body tightened in response. He diverted his attention to the next button, and the next.

"I'm curious, Sara. Did you *peg* West by the way he parts his hair or was it something more complicated, like the shine on his shoes?"

"That really bothers you, doesn't it? The fact that I could know so much about you just through observation."

"What bothers me is your safety, not the idea that you made a few guesses that happened to be fairly accurate. Jumping to conclusions like that could one day get you in more trouble than you can handle."

Her laughter was a slight movement beneath his fingers, a soft echo of her amusement. "It works both ways, you know. I could be planning to drive you outside of town and rob you."

"You wouldn't do that."

"Are you sure?"

"Yes."

"How do you know?"

"Well, for one thing I have Cleo to protect me. And for another, you've already decided that I have nothing worth stealing."

"I wouldn't want to upset Cleo. It's obvious she holds you in the highest regard."

"It's mutual, believe me."

"What do the two of you have in common, other than the call of the wild?"

"We both loved the same woman."

"Loved? In the past tense?"

"Definitely past."

"What happened to her?"

"She left us behind when she accepted a better job in another city and a no-pets-allowed apartment. I'm not sure either one of us actually missed her all that much once she was gone, but it became something of a grudge match to see who possessed the greater tolerance and which one would leave first. So far, it's a stalemate."

"Interesting. Any chance of a cessation of hostilities?"

"Not likely." The last button eased from the loop, and the dress parted to reveal the long, smooth slope of her back. Ben thought seriously about running his palm across it, slipping his hand beneath the lace and satin, reaching around to cup her breast and expose her intuition for the foolishness it was. Maybe if he'd been in a better position to control the van, he might have taken on the task of demonstrating the danger in making presumptions. "You're unbuttoned," he said, reaching around her to grasp the steering wheel with his left hand and her elbow with his right. "Now, take your foot off that accelerator and let me drive."

"Thanks. I will be so glad to get into my own clothes." She pushed against him with a wiry strength as she levered up and off, balancing with one foot in the other seat while she gathered up the bulky satin skirt and squeezed between the seats into the back of the van. "I owe you for this."

"A hundred bucks." He settled behind the wheel and slowed the van to an acceptable speed.

"Plus tips. Of course, you never know how those will run, especially at a private party."

"Isn't it slightly inhospitable to expect guests to tip the bartender?"

"West doesn't *expect* the guests to tip. Some of them just do, that's all."

Ben considered the defensive note in her voice. The rustle of satin whisked behind him, and he looked in the rearview mirror just in time to see the wedding gown part in a deep V, revealing her back all the way down to the elastic band of her brief bikini panties. There were no bra straps to mar the view, and he admired her ivory skin until a car horn brought him back from the edge of fantasy. But his gaze strayed to the rearview mirror again at the first opportunity.

"You'll need to watch for Mayflower Road," she said matter-of-factly, and he ripped his gaze from the mirror to check the nearest street sign.

"Nice neighborhood," he commented, noting the widening of the streets and the increasing number of stately homes behind wrought-iron gates.

"I know. I'm planning to live here."

"With West."

"That's the plan. Oh, no! Give me that! Let go! I said, *let go!*"

Cleo's playful growl preceded the sound of an ominous rip. Ben glanced back to see Sara struggling to pull something away from the dog. "What was that?"

"My dress." Even at a distance, it was clear the words were delivered through clenched teeth.

"She tore the wedding dress?" A car pulled in front of him, and he couldn't spare another glance. "How bad is it?" he asked with genuine concern. "Did she ruin it?"

"Oh, yes. It's ruined, all right."

He looked over his shoulder. Sara was turned toward him, the ivory dress drooping in an uneven line around her shoulders, a soggy strip of black in each hand. Cleo sat at her feet, looking pleased by her part in this latest game. "What's that?"

"My black silk dress."

Relief washed over him with the knowledge that he wouldn't have to explain how his dog managed to destroy a million-dollar gown. "She didn't tear the wedding dress?"

"No such luck. She had to mangle the only thing I ever paid full retail for...and I never even got to wear it."

"I'm sorry," he said. "I'll pay to replace it."

"You can't afford to do that, Ben. I spent far too much money on it to begin with...but thanks. It was a nice gesture."

He heard the rich rustle of the satin and looked in the rearview mirror to see her holding the bodice of the wedding gown in place as she frowned at the scraps of black silk on the van floor. She looked up, caught his gaze and sighed. "I hate it when a plan falls apart."

Ben wanted badly to cheer her up. "I may be over-rating my intuitive abilities here, but I can tell by the arch of your eyebrows that you're already formulating a new plan."

She adjusted the ivory lace covering her arms and sagging on her shoulders. "Considering the extent of my wardrobe at the moment, the only plan I have is to have you button up the back of this dress again."

"I could turn this jalopy around. We'd be back at your house in twenty minutes or less."

"Only if we collected another speeding ticket on the way. At best, it would take an hour to get there and back. And that doesn't include time for any unscheduled stops or wild-key chases."

"So do we proceed on to the West Ridgeman home?"

"We're almost there, and one way or another, I'm going to be at this party."

"A woman after my own heart," he said and was surprised to realize he meant it.

"The next intersection will be Mayflower. Turn left." She walked to the front, holding the gown in place with one hand and placing the other on the back of his seat for balance. After he completed the turn, she pointed at a pair of large, elaborate, open gates at the end of the block. "That's the house. Follow the drive all the way around. We'll park in back. Just wave at the valet as we pass. He'll recognize the van."

"Any idea what we'll do when we get there?"

"Not yet." Sara stooped, propping her arms on the seat backs as the Ridgeman estate came into view. "But I'll think of something."

Chapter Four

"Are you sure you want me to do this?"

Hands on her hips, Sara looked at the shadowed balcony of the second story. "Unless you'd rather climb the trellis and tap on that window."

"Depends on whose window it is."

"I don't know. I've never been upstairs."

Ben turned his head to look at her. "You're going to marry this guy and you've never been in his bedroom?"

"How do you know his bedroom isn't downstairs? Now, keep your mind on earning your salary and go on up to the door and knock."

"What if he answers?"

"Improvise."

"Right." He pantomimed a knock. "Hello, Mr. Ridgeman. I'll be your bartender this evening, but could you introduce me to your sister first because I want to borrow her clothes." He smiled at Sara. "Think that will do it?"

"I think so, yes." She returned his smile with saccharine assurance. "You should say it exactly like that if West answers the door—which he won't. Now go on before someone comes outside and sees me in this wedding dress.''

Ben studied the well-lighted terrace he had to cross to reach the kitchen door. ''Tell me again why this is a better plan than returning to your house to change clothes.''

''It would have taken too long.''

He nodded. ''Right.''

Her sigh was deeply frustrated. ''Okay, so maybe I made a poor choice, but we're here now and I know DeeNee will help me. Just say whatever you have to say to get her outside.''

''You're sure she's here?''

''The only thing I'm sure about is that I'm crouched behind a boxwood hedge, hoping the sprinkler system isn't set to come on in the next fifteen minutes.''

Ben couldn't recall the last time he'd been so well entertained. ''You could have stayed in the van with Cleo.''

''I'll take my chances with the sprinkler, thanks. Now, go on.''

He made a production of checking the area. ''Okay,'' he said, talking covertly from the side of his mouth. ''Cover me, I'm going in.''

A twig hit him square between the shoulder blades, and he was glad she didn't have access to more advanced weapons. With an easy stride, he mounted the terrace steps and approached the glass-paned door. After rapping lightly on the panes, he waited for someone to answer.

A tall, dour-faced man opened the door. ''Yes?''

Ben smiled broadly. ''Hello,'' he said. ''I'm At Your Service.''

The man evaluated Ben in a single, unimpressed glance. "I sincerely doubt it." And he closed the door.

Ben looked at Sara and shrugged. She motioned and he knocked again.

The door opened to impart the butler's scowl. "*May* I help you?"

"As a matter of fact, I'm here to help you. I'm a bartender."

"I don't drink." The door closed.

Ben looked to the shrub for guidance.

She stood up and brushed away a twig. "That's Arthur. I don't know what he's doing in the kitchen, but we'll never get past him. Not with you looking like you just fell off a turnip truck. I'll have to think of something else."

"I'll have you know there is nothing about me that resembles a turnip."

"Tell that to Arthur."

Ben walked across the terrace and down the steps. "Does your beau know Arthur is answering his door?"

"That's what West pays him to do. He's the butler." She scrutinized the trellis, from the ground to the balcony. "Can you climb that?"

He pursed his lips. "I could. The question is, would I?"

"Well, would you?"

"Depends on what kind of motivation I had."

"My gratitude?"

"For that, I might be able to throw a couple of pebbles and hit the window."

"As if we could find a pebble of any kind in this lawn."

"Oh, there's bound to be something. Look around."

"No. This is ridiculous. I'm just going to walk in there and act like this is the dress I planned to wear. If West sees me, he will just have to deal with it."

Ben liked the sound of that. "Are you going to tell him the dress twinkled at you?"

"You're enjoying this, aren't you?"

"I can see the humorous side."

She squared her shoulders and smoothed the front of the wedding gown. "I just hope the joke isn't on me."

SARA DIDN'T BOTHER to knock. She simply opened the door and breezed into the kitchen like a hurricane heading for shore. "Hello, Arthur." She addressed the scowling butler in a pleasant, don't-mess-with-me tone. "This is Ben. He'll be in charge of the bar this evening. He needs something else to wear. Would you be so kind as to find something suitable for him, please?"

A fly under a microscope couldn't have come under closer scrutiny. Ben fully expected the butler to take a magnifying glass from his pocket and check for dirt behind his ears. "If you'll pardon my saying so, Miss Gunnerson, it would be simpler to outfit the Rockettes."

"Oh, but not nearly as much fun." Ben defended his dignity and his camouflage vest. "I've been told my high kick is a wonder to behold."

Arthur's glower was a beauty. "I'm certain it is a spectacle. However—"

"Come on, Arthur, be a sport." Sara rushed to interrupt. "I know you can dig up something for him. You're a genius with fashion."

The dour expression softened a degree and then he took a second look at Sara. "I hope you don't expect me to *dig up* something for you, too. Genius has its limits."

A slight stiffening of her posture was her only perceptible sign of tension, and Ben wasn't sure he would have noticed if he hadn't been watching for it. "I don't expect you to tax your creativity for me, Arthur. Where's DeeNee?"

"Miss DeeNee went home to change for the party." Arthur's gaze ran disparagingly over the wedding gown, making the clear implication that Sara should have done the same.

"How long ago did she leave?"

"Twenty, possibly thirty minutes ago."

"She's going to be late for the party," Ben said for Sara's benefit. "But then, it might be worth it to arrive properly dressed."

Sara smiled testily. "I'll call her while you're changing into something else."

"You're sure I can't just wear my own duds?"

"Not in this house," Arthur said crisply. "Those *duds* would have to be taken into the next county before I would feel comfortable burying them." Turning on his heel he walked, stiff and starched, to the kitchen stairway. "If you will follow me, G.I. Joe...."

Ben raised his eyebrows and fell into step behind the butler. "I like you, Art. You can call me G. And, strictly as a matter of information, the salesman at the Military Surplus Store assured me these pants were worn by General Schwartzkopf, himself. I wouldn't put on just any pair of dungarees to come to a swank party like this, you know."

Arthur marched up the stairs and Ben stayed right on his heels.

"DEENEE." Sara cupped her hand around the mouthpiece of the kitchen phone to prevent Annette and Clark—the husband and wife servers who were conspicuously eavesdropping—from overhearing the conversation. "Listen. I need a dress. Can you bring one for me?"

"What happened to the black silk you told me about?"

"A dog ate it."

DeeNee's voice bubbled with mirth. "A canine with designer tastes. I can't wait to hear the rest of this."

"Can you bring something?" Sara allowed desperation to creep into her voice. "And the sooner you can get here with it, the better."

"Actually, I was thinking about not coming back. You know how much I detest these boring affairs West insists upon calling parties. However, if you are running around my brother's house with no clothes on, it might be worth the trip over. Are you?"

Sara turned her back to Annette, who was easing closer under the guise of looking for another serving tray. "Am I what?" she whispered.

"Running naked in West's house."

"Of course not," Sara's voice came up to full volume. "I just need something to wear."

"What's wrong with what you have on? If you're not naked, you must be wearing something." DeeNee, like West, could be tenacious to the point of annihilation.

Sara turned again and reduced her tone to a hoarse whisper. "I'm wearing a wedding gown."

"What? Talk louder. I can't hear you."

She gave up on discretion. "I said, I'm wearing a wedding gown." Something Annette had, undoubtedly, figured out for herself anyway.

There was a brief pause on the other end of the line. "Is there going to be a wedding?"

"No. I put this dress on by accident and—"

DeeNee's laughter came through loud and clear. "You don't do anything by accident, Sara. This is some kind of practical joke, isn't it? Some wonderful little plan you have to bring my big, stiff-necked brother to his knees, right?"

"Just bring anything you think will fit me and get here as fast as you can." Slamming the phone into the cradle, she turned to face the curious, expectant stares of Clark and Annette.

"THERE IS NO WAY to make these fit." Ben thought it should be obvious that his thirty-four-inch waist was not going to squeeze into Arthur's size thirty-one trousers. "And my shoes have to be twelves. I cannot wear anything smaller. No matter how many times you assure me I can."

The butler looked unimpressed. "I have done as requested and found you something appropriate to wear. It is entirely your choice to wear it or not."

"Good. I'll borrow this shirt, that bow tie and those suspenders." He pointed out his choices from the collection in Arthur's closet. "But I'll keep my pants on."

It was clear that Arthur wasn't big on compromise. "That, of course, is your decision. However, I doubt Mr. West will consider it good judgment."

"I'll stay behind the bar, and he'll never know whether or not I'm wearing any pants."

A slight breach occurred in the butler's stern facade, the faint hint of a smile. "As you wish." Arthur picked out the selected items and handed them to Ben. "If I may say so, sir, you have expensive taste in accessories. The tie is a D'Lur original."

Ben looped the ends of the tie around his neck. "I know, and as I'm sure you're aware, not just any bow tie would complement these dungarees." He pushed one arm through the sleeve of the starched white shirt taken fresh from the butler's vast collection of starched white shirts, heard the rip of a seam and looked at the damage before turning to Arthur with an apologetic shrug. "Maybe he won't notice that I'm not wearing a shirt, either."

Like a schoolmaster weary of dealing with a difficult student, the butler held out his hand for the torn garment. "I will get a larger shirt for you from Mr. West's wardrobe. Kindly wait here."

Ben kindly waited.

"I'LL PARK IT MYSELF, thanks." DeeNee Ridgeman dismissed the valet with a wave of her hand and sped past a row of parked cars to the rear of the house. She pulled up beside the At Your Service van, braked and released the clutch all in one continuous and practiced routine. "We're back where we started, Brody," she said to the black-faced pug in the passenger seat. "At least we know the food will be good, huh?" She rubbed the dog's ear. "I promise, though, that if this party is as dull as the last one, you won't have to attend any more for the rest of the summer."

The pug wheezed and licked her hand with his long, pink tongue.

"Let's go see what that silly Sara has up her sleeve, shall we?" DeeNee held out her arms and Brody jumped into them, licking her chin with roughly textured adoration. "Okay, okay." She opened the car door and set the pug on the ground before frowning at her brother's soaring modern Grecian and utterly pretentious residence. "This had better be worth the trip," she muttered.

Agreement came from behind her in an unexpected and friendly bark. DeeNee glanced over her shoulder and into the lustrous, hopeful eyes of a black Labrador retriever. "Hello there," she said. "What are you doing in Sara's van?"

The dog wagged from one end to the other.

With an easy motion and an easier smile, DeeNee stepped out of her low-slung sports car and moved closer to the window of the van. Placing her palm against the glass, she smiled when the Lab pushed its nose against the other side in response. "You look too intelligent to eat a nasty old dress."

Three soft barks clearly indicated a plea of innocent, a willingness to be friends and a request for release. DeeNee didn't have to think twice. "You want out of there, don't you? It's too hot to be locked up in a stuffy old van, no matter what crime you committed." She patted the glass, then moved to the back and tried the door. It opened with one pull, and the dog jumped down, her tail swaying like a metronome,

rhythmically delighted to be paroled. "Hello."
DeeNee stroked the dog's head and scratched under
the noble chin. "Aren't you a sweetheart," she murmured. "Brody, where did you go? Come back here
and meet our new friend."

The pug's snuffle preceded his stroll around the van,
and he pranced right up to the new arrival. In moments, the dogs had sniffed, postured and made
peace. They took off in a rambling run. "Stay in Uncle
West's yard," she called after them, knowing there
was no way over, under or through the iron bars and
brick walls that sectioned off the property from the
surrounding neighborhood. West was adamant about
security, and while DeeNee didn't think he had to be
quite so paranoid, she liked being able to turn Brody
loose without having to supervise his every move. Her
brother, she knew, wished she would leave the pug at
home.

Hoping against hope she wasn't about to waste yet
another perfectly good evening, she walked across the
terrace and approached the kitchen door.

SARA DUSTED HER HANDS and tried to look as if she
had her life under control. "Well," she said. "It looks
like everything is ready. I don't know what I'd do
without the two of you."

Annette and Clark nodded a polite thank-you, but
Sara could feel their curiosity pressing her against the
wall, and she answered with a fading smile. Whatever
had possessed her to put on this wedding dress? Why
hadn't she gone home to change when she had the
chance? And where was DeeNee? "I, uh, think I'll go
upstairs and see how the bartender's new clothes

look." She backed toward the kitchen stairs, stepped on the bridal train and almost tripped. She caught herself in time, though, and jerked the yards of satin up and out of her way. "Annette?" She tried to sound as if there was nothing out of the ordinary, as if she was accustomed to scooping up bridal trains before she walked up a flight of stairs. "Make sure there's enough ice and napkins on the bar. And Clark, you could check on the, uh...oh, just think of something and go check on it."

Bunching the heavy satin in her fists, Sara headed up the stairs. She'd hardly turned the corner of the landing when she heard the swoosh of the swinging door opening from the dining room into the kitchen.

"Has anyone seen Sara?"

It was West's voice, and she didn't wait to hear what Clark or Annette answered. She fled up the stairs like a mouse scurrying at the first tinkle of the cat's bell. At the top of the steps, a narrow hall led to a closed door, which she opened, taking care to be quiet as she slipped inside. She gathered the seemingly endless yards of satin around her, closed the door to within a fraction of latching and listened for the sound of approaching footsteps.

"Hi."

Ben's whisper warmed her ear and nearly startled Sara out of her skin. As she spun to face him, the door shut with an ominously loud click. "What are you doing in here?" she whispered.

"Waiting for Arthur," he whispered back. "What are you doing in here?"

"Running from West."

"I thought you wanted him to catch you."

"Not in this dress."

"What happened to the idea that West will have to deal with your choice of party duds?"

"So, okay, when push comes to shove, I'm a coward."

"Me, too."

Sara's heartbeat skittered with the sudden, irrefutable awareness that not only was Ben bare-chested, but the nearness of his bare chest to her seemed to be causing some difficulty with her breathing. "What will I do if he comes up here?"

The whisper had scarcely passed her lips when West called up the stairs. "Sara? Where are you?"

Ben looked at the door. "I think he's coming up here."

She looked at Ben. "I'm going to hide."

"Good plan. In the closet? Under the bed?"

"The closet. I don't think I can get this dress under the bed."

"Sara?" Footsteps thudded softly on the stairs. "Are you up here, Sara?"

Ben moved to the closet and opened the door with a flourish. "Quick. In here."

"I can't believe I'm doing this," she mumbled as she swept across the butler's bedroom and into his closet. Ben pushed and pummeled the train in after her, then stepped in and closed them into a still, cloistered darkness just as West opened the outer door.

"Sara?"

"Mr. West?"

"Arthur?"

"Shh." Sara put her finger to her lips even though it was black as sin inside the closet.

"I didn't say anything," Ben whispered directly and very softly into her ear.

Velvet couldn't have been any softer, Sara thought with a tiny, treacherous shiver of attraction. "Shh," was all she could manage to say as she tried not to think about how close his bare chest was to her now. Or how close she was to being discovered in a closet standing close to his bare chest.

"I'm looking for Sara," West's voice explained on the other side of the closet door. "Have you seen her?"

"She was in the kitchen earlier," Arthur's voice answered.

"That maid woman said she came up here."

"Why would she do that, sir?"

"I can't imagine, but if you see her, tell her I'm looking for her."

Sara shifted her weight from one foot to the other... and bumped up against the unmistakable curve of Ben's body in front of her. She could hear him breathing, feel their body heat mingling in the confined air of the closet. All right. So she'd known there was a physical attraction the moment she opened her eyes on the porch and met the sexy confidence in his. And now she knew that hiding in a closet with him was not conducive to clear thinking. However, since she operated on the theory that knowing was half the battle, she should be in good shape. The moment they were out of this forced togetherness, she'd forget all about this stifling longing to touch his chest... just touch it. She didn't want to run her fingers across it or anything like that. A touch would suffice, just enough to confirm her suspicion that he was in prime physical condition.

"Shall I look for her, sir?" Arthur asked.

"No. She'll turn up. This is one party she does not want to miss." West's voice turned away, then became stronger on the last two words as if he had turned back. "You should be at the door, Arthur. The guests will be arriving any moment, and I want you there to greet them."

"I'll hang up this shirt and be right down."

"Good man."

The sound of the outer door closing carried into the closet, and Sara breathed a sigh of relief. West was leaving. And he hadn't seen her. Thank heaven for small favors. The knob on the closet door turned with a small squeak.

"Oh, and Arthur, I want you to check the—" West was suddenly back in the room as the closet door began to open.

Sara elbowed Ben out of the way and grabbed the knob. The door bounced shut.

"What's wrong with your closet?" West interrupted himself to ask.

"The door appears to be stuck." Arthur tugged on the doorknob, and Sara held on for dear life, creating a bumping match of door against doorframe.

"That's odd," West said. "Let me give you a hand."

Her heart leaped to her throat. She was about to be discovered. In a closet. In a wedding dress. With a bare-chested man. Grasping the door with both hands, she braced for disaster.

"Pull on the count of three, Arthur."

The pressure built.

"One, two..."

Ben's arms slipped around her, on either side, and his hands closed over hers. In a split second, the odds shifted in her favor, and she leaned gratefully into his strength.

"Three."

Their resistance held, and Sara allowed herself to appreciate the supple vitality in the muscular arms pressed against her sides.

"Hmm. It does seem to be jammed, doesn't it?" West's voice snapped Sara out of her moment of inappropriate and lustful appreciation.

"I will make arrangements to have someone fix it tomorrow," Arthur said.

Sara could feel West's puzzled gaze on the door, could well imagine his frown. He had no tolerance for doors that jammed or anything that didn't operate with smooth efficiency. When she realized Ben's fingers were loosening their grip over hers, she caught his hand and placed it on the doorknob.

Sure enough, West tried the door one more time. "Very odd," he said.

"I'll take care of it." Arthur's voice faded as he walked away from the closet. A moment later, the outer door opened with a quiet whoosh. "What was it you wanted me to check, Mr. West?"

"I've forgotten for the moment, Arthur." West sounded distracted as he turned from the closet. "I'm certain you've already taken care of all the minor details, anyway. I'll go downstairs with you. I should keep looking for Sara. I wanted to talk to her before the guests arrived, but I guess it will have to wait."

"I'm certain you'll find her, sir."

Their voices ebbed, and when the bedroom door closed, the sound was reduced first to a low vibration and then to silence. Sara sagged in relief and slowly released her grip on the doorknob. Ben's hands stayed over hers as she drew back, and when her hands rested against the lace and satin covering her waist, she found herself in the circle of his arms, her back pressed against his chest, her head resting beneath his chin.

"Shh." His whispered warning was the only sound in the darkness, his breath an echo of her own escalating awareness. She knew if she tried to move away, he would caution her to wait a little longer. She knew if she assured him West was gone, he would advise her to wait a little longer. She knew if she made the slightest protest, he would let her go...and she would wish she had waited a little longer.

"I'm pretty sure we're alone now." She breathed out the words over a rush of internal protests. Her body liked the protective warmth of his wrapped around her, despite the meticulous intrusion of her better judgment. She barely knew Ben Northcross, and what she did know made her certain she did not want to get involved with him. That was the trouble with sexual attractions. They were so seldom discriminating in their choice, and almost never resulted in a good match outside of the bedroom...or closet. "We should probably get out of here," she said.

"No doubt about it," he answered.

"West is gone now and—" she lost her train of thought as he traced a fingertip along her neckline "—you're not wearing a shirt."

"I like this dress. What do you suppose would happen if it twinkled at me?"

That did it. Sara groped for the doorknob. "You'd get pixie dust in your eyes. Let's go. I have things to do, and getting out of this dress is first on the list."

Ben reached past her and pushed open the door. "All right, pixie, let's get to it."

Sara started through the doorway but had to stop and maneuver about half of the satin skirt out ahead of her before she could fit. "Unbutton me," she said.

"Haven't we been through this already?"

"Yes. Now do it again."

"You didn't use the magic word."

"Ben, please."

"That isn't the magic word. It's twink—"

"*Don't* say that."

"Okay. We'll change the word to sparkle. Do you like that better?"

"Just unbutton me and keep your sense of humor to yourself."

His fingers touched the back of her neck, and a shiver of heated response raced right down her spine. She pretended it was nerves.

"What would you have said if Ridgeman had opened that door?" His tone was casual, light, with just the right touch of companionable curiosity to inspire a reply.

"I don't know," she answered. "He wouldn't have believed me no matter what I said. Not with you standing half naked behind me."

"Mmm, I hadn't thought of that. And what's worse, I'm wearing camouflage pants, so he might have surmised I wasn't wearing anything at all and punched me in the nose."

"He might have surmised he could sue you for being in his closet."

"But I was there strictly in the line of duty."

"I thought it was because you were a coward like me."

"That, too. You'll vouch for me, won't you?"

"That would be easier if you'd put on some clothes."

"First you want me to take them off, then you want me to put them on. Besides, I am wearing a tie." His fingers moved to the middle of her back. "It's a D'Lur original, too."

"That will impress West. Why aren't you wearing a shirt? And something other than those dungarees?"

"I ripped Arthur's shirt and he went to get another one. And the dungarees stay. Arthur and I are not the same size around the waist, in case you didn't notice."

"I've been a little distracted this evening, and frankly, the size of your waist hasn't been on my mind."

"A pity. I've been thinking I could just about put my hands around yours."

"Only if I stopped breathing. Could you hurry with those buttons?"

"Sure thing. My fingers are getting calluses already from buttoning you out and in and out of this dress."

"Well, this will be the last time, believe me."

He worked his way to her waist. "So, what are you going to wear to this party?"

"DeeNee's bringing a dress for me."

He paused. "Do you want me to button this back up until she gets here?"

"No. Just finish the buttons and then you can go on downstairs and get acquainted with your place behind the bar. As soon as you put on a shirt, that is."

"Looks like we're in the same fix. I'm waiting for a shirt and you're waiting for a dress."

"I think that's the shirt on the bed." She indicated a crisply starched white shirt hanging from the bedpost. "Arthur must have left it for you."

"Lucky me," Ben said dryly. "Just when I was beginning to think I'd have some reward for all this unbuttoning."

"You will be amply rewarded. A paycheck plus tips, remember?"

The floor in the hallway creaked, and Sara looked toward the door in a panic. "They're coming back," she whispered sharply as she gathered her skirts. "Get in the closet."

"I should be getting overtime for this." Holding her dress together—Ben's hands at her shoulders, hers at the waist—they shuffled sideways toward the closet. The train caught on the heel of Sara's pump and she fell backward, knocking Ben onto the bed with a startled whumph. The unbuttoned back of the wedding gown parted as she landed on top of him, and her bare back pressed his bare chest into the mattress. She struggled to get up, but the top of the dress pinned her shoulders, the skirt bunched around her ankles, and Ben's efforts to help her get upright all conspired to keep her flat against him. "Be still," he whispered. "Listen."

She did, and heard a portentous quiet on the other side of the bedroom door. If West opened that door now and saw her half out of the wedding gown, rolling around on the bed with a half-dressed man in camouflage pants, he would not be amused. He'd be furious, especially when he found out Ben was the bartender. Her mind tossed options like a Caesar salad and blended them into crisp panic. There was no way to run, no place to hide, no—

But West didn't know she was wearing a wedding dress. And if he didn't see her face . . .

Impulsively, she rolled over and, grabbing the ends of the D'Lur Original, she pulled Ben on top of her.

"Wha—"

Before he could finish the word, she kissed him.

Chapter Five

The kiss got off to a rough start. Mainly because Ben was accustomed to having at least some warning that a kiss was imminent. Of course, with Sara, he was beginning to think there was never much warning. She drove too fast, talked too fast, rushed around making plans and then abruptly changing them when they went awry. Even now, her lips were in a hurry and missed a good portion of his. Once he got them aligned, however, the kiss improved considerably. He managed to slow things down, persuaded her to linger a little and taste just how pleasurable a moment could be.

That the pleasure exceeded even his expectations fascinated him, and he became so immersed in the sensation that he barely heard the soft tapping on the door and the softer murmur of a woman's voice in the hallway. He didn't think Sara heard it at all, because her grip on the ends of his tie didn't slacken. Neither did the enchanting response of her lips beneath the pressure of his.

Ben had no idea who had knocked on the door or who she had been seeking. Arthur could have a girlfriend for all he knew. At the moment, he was just glad the butler had had the foresight to lock the door when he left. Otherwise, someone would have seen more than they should: two people, a man and a woman, wrapped in a tangle of satin and dungarees, bare chest and bare back, lips that fused into a surprisingly heated kiss. Sara would deny feeling any heat, he knew, but she had gotten more out of this impulsive act than she'd bargained for and he decided to insist that she admit it.

When she pulled away with a quickly indrawn and quivery breath, he was ready for her.

"I hope you realize what you just did," he said.

Her eyes widened and lost a wisp of their dreamy darkness. "W-what?"

"You kissed me."

"I *know* that."

"You used my lips for your own convenience."

"I didn't want West to see—"

"That is immaterial. You kissed me, Ms. Gunnerson, for your own purpose and without regard for my feelings."

"Your feelings and your lips didn't seem to mind a moment ago."

"I'm a male. It takes a few minutes for my lips to figure out what emotion I'm feeling."

Her lips pursed. "And now that they have figured it out, they're outraged?"

"Let's just say you may have done irreparable harm to my self-esteem."

"It was only a kiss."

"Uh-huh." He nodded, leading her further along the path to reprisal. "And what if I had been the one to initiate it? Would it have been *only a kiss,* then?"

"If you thought you were about to be discovered in a compromising situation by the person you intended to marry, I think I could be understanding about it, yes."

"So if I ever find myself in bed with you and in danger of being caught by my future wife, I have your consent to hide behind your lips?"

"That isn't what I said." But she sounded unsure. "I said I could be understanding."

"Oh. So you would understand if I kissed you."

"That isn't what I said, either."

The breathless quality in her voice pleased him altogether too much. "Hmm. Let me get this clear. I can kiss you—but only if I need to."

"No—er, yes. But only if it's necessary."

Cornered. He smiled. "Oh, believe me, it is absolutely necessary."

She looked at him, all eyes and emotion and curiosity. That was one characteristic he had already come to love about Sara. No matter how much she knew what she wanted and what she didn't want, she was curious about what she might miss.

So Ben made sure she saw his intent, forced her eyes to do battle with his and concede his point that it hadn't been just a kiss at all. Lowering his head, he let his intention kindle her anticipation, heighten her awareness and allow her plenty of time to realize she could protest, that she had the power to stop this encounter in its tracks.

She didn't, and when his mouth closed over hers, there was a soft sigh of discovery, the sensual mingling of lips and breath and unbidden desires. She deserved this, he thought. If only because she had taken one look at him and blithely pegged him as a nice guy who represented no danger to her.

Well, her intuition wasn't worth a wooden nickel to her at the moment. And just to emphasize his point, he increased the intensity of the caress, insisting that she respond simply because it suited him to prove that he could. He feathered tiny kisses all along the line of her lips, finding unexpected delight in the pliable curve at the corner of her mouth. His lips just fit there, as if that single spot had been dimpled just for him.

He kissed her with all the expertise at his command, and just as he decided to leave her wanting more, she flattened both palms against his chest and shoved him over. If he'd been expecting the move, of course, she couldn't have done it, but she surprised him, and the next thing he knew, he was flat on his back with an acre of wedding gown billowing around him and an irate woman sitting on his chest.

"All right, Casanova, let that be a lesson to you. When it comes to kissing, a woman can be just as insincere as a man. And the next time you try to prove some macho point to me, you'd better think twice."

Ben was enchanted. "Punk."

She blinked. "What?"

"Punk," he repeated. "Your threat needed a punch line. Something to give it a little more oomph. Punk seemed appropriate. You know..." He did a fair imitation of Clint Eastwood. "You'd better think twice... *punk.*"

With her reluctant smile, the anger—although Ben preferred to think of it as passion—vanished. "All right, Mr. Macho. I concede this round to you. But only because I don't have time to debate."

"It's a good thing."

"Afraid you'd lose?"

"Afraid I'd have to teach you the difference between insincere and honest, and that could take so long, I might not clear a hundred bucks tonight."

There was a flicker of challenge in her eyes, followed quickly by a gleam of bravado. "Plus tips."

He nodded. "Plus tips."

She moved off him, her satin-wrapped thighs brushing across his bare skin with unintentional but irresistible impact. "Go downstairs, Ben, before you become any more delusional. And for heaven's sake, put on that shirt."

"What are you going to put on?"

"DeeNee will be here any minute with something."

"What if she isn't?"

Sara displayed the full weight of a frown as she sat on the side of the bed and looked at him. "She will be, don't worry. Just get behind the bar and act like you know what you're doing."

"If I leave you alone and she doesn't show, you'll be stuck in Arthur's room wearing a partially unbuttoned dress."

"One way or another, I'll be at the party, Ben. And I won't be wearing this dress, buttoned or unbuttoned."

"Okay." He got to his feet and pulled on his second crisp white shirt of the evening. It fit much better this time. "See you below." He made certain the door locked behind him. Then he trotted down the kitchen stairs, fastening his shirt and knotting his D'Lur original as he went.

SARA LEANED out the window and searched the dusk for signs of rescue. If DeeNee didn't get here soon with that change of clothes, she might as well throw herself off the ledge. Of course, she was only on the second floor, and the lawn below was so lush, the only injuries she was likely to sustain were scraped knees and unsightly grass stains. However, jumping would be something of a symbolic gesture. A cathartic means of demonstrating her opinion of the evening thus far.

With a frown, she turned her back to the window and began working with the buttons that ran from elbow to wrist on the lace sleeves. She had sent Ben off to tend bar without a second thought, never considering she would have any trouble with the rest of the buttons or be unable to get out of the wedding dress on her own. How she had ever gotten herself fastened in the gown, she'd never know, because the buttons seemed to require two hands and total concentration. She hadn't freed herself by so much as a quarter inch since he left, and if DeeNee didn't show up soon...

A flicker of light darted across the room and, like a lightning bug on a June night, twinkled for an instant and was gone.

Looking up, Sara caught sight of herself in the mirror. Like a toddler delighted by her own reflection, she began to smile. Really, the dress was lovely and she was lovely in it. Why hadn't she wanted West to see her wearing it? She moved toward the dresser, wishing the mirror was larger so she could see exactly how the train draped behind her. And whatever had made her leave the veil on her bed at home? The wedding gown wasn't complete without it. How could Ben know she was... No, not Ben. How could West fall under her spell if... No, not West.

She tried to frown, but the smile on her lips seemed to be as much a part of her as the dimple at the corner of her mouth. A giddy laugh lurked just behind her eyes, and happiness nestled inside her like a present, all wrapped and waiting to be opened. It was an extraordinary feeling, and she wanted to share it with someone, anyone—Ben. And just like that, he was there. Standing beside her, wearing the same smile, looking roguishly handsome in his tuxedo...

Tuxedo?

"Sara?" The sound of her name was accompanied by a soft rapping noise, and with a blink she turned to look at the closed door. "Sara?" The voice and the noise came a second time before she could get her feet in motion and move away from the mirror. Feeling slightly disoriented, she turned the knob and opened the door.

"Sara! Have you been in here all this time? I knocked and knocked, but—" DeeNee Ridgeman stopped talking and stared at her for a moment, and then her irrepressible laughter bubbled all over the room. "I thought you were joking, but you really are wearing a wedding gown."

Sara's spirits took a flying leap off cloud nine and landed in a mess of reality. "I cannot believe it," she said, realizing what she had done while standing in front of the mirror. "I have buttoned myself back in this dress." Grabbing DeeNee by the arm, she pulled her into Arthur's room and closed the door. "Unbutton me, and no matter what happens, do not let me look in that mirror."

"YOU'RE RELIEVED."

Ben looked over his shoulder at a solemn-faced Arthur. "I didn't know I was worried."

"I have been sent to replace you," Arthur stated formally.

"Can't be done. I'm the only one of my kind."

The butler might have frowned, but it was hard to tell. "Ms. Gunnerson requests your presence in my bedroom immediately. I have been asked to tend to the dispersement of beverages in your absence. Do you have any questions?"

Dropping the bar towel on the bar, Ben admired Arthur's poker-straight properness. "How would you like to come to work for me, Art?"

"I wouldn't think you had any need for a butler...sir."

The way he was able to say *sir* and make it sound like it had a nasty smell was masterful.

"I haven't up until now, but your charm is winning me over. What do you say, Artie?"

Arthur picked up the towel and folded it into a precise, three-crease fold with ends that lined up perfectly. "I dislike to belabor the obvious, but you cannot afford my services."

"Hmm." Ben considered that with a frown. "How do you know I'm not Howard Hughes's nephew?"

"He was an only child," Arthur replied without missing a beat. "You are expected upstairs, and I believe Ms. Gunnerson does not like to be kept waiting."

"You got that right. Patience is definitely not her strong suit." Ben turned on his heel and headed for the kitchen.

"WHY IN THE HELL did you do this?" He stared in astonishment at the row of buttons, all neatly secured in their corresponding loops, which ran from Sara's neckline to the middle of her butt. "When I left, all but the bottom third of these were undone. You could have slipped the dress over your head and been out of it."

"I realize that," Sara said tightly. "Will you please just unbutton me?"

"I'm getting blisters on my fingers from getting you in and out of this dress. If I have to file for workers' comp, you won't have a leg to stand on."

"How many times have you done this?" DeeNee Ridgeman sat cross-legged on Arthur's bed, watching the activity with interest.

Sara had provided brusque introductions between jerking Ben inside the room and telling him to unbutton her again. Impatience should have been her middle name.

"I have to tell you," DeeNee continued. "I tried everything to get the dress undone. I even tried to cut the loops with a butcher knife."

Ben winced at the thought of the million-dollar dress after such surgery. Thank goodness he wouldn't have to explain that to Pop. "I don't know why it's so difficult. All you have to do is gently slip the loop over the button, like this." He demonstrated, and DeeNee leaned forward to watch.

"I tried that," she said. "Didn't work."

"Here, I'll show you again." He grasped Sara by the shoulders. "Turn this way."

"Not *that* way," DeeNee and Sara said in tandem.

"Away from the mirror." DeeNee sat back on the bed. "She can't bear to look at herself. Don't ask me why. I think the dress is wildly flattering."

"I agree. She looks great in it."

"Will you stop admiring this voodoo dress and get me out of it?"

"Voodoo?" DeeNee repeated.

"She means magic." Ben worked another button free of its loop. "The dress twink— Ow!"

Sara stepped off his instep, and he bent to rub it. "Would you get on with it?" she asked. "I am not going to miss any more of this party because of some meaningless chitchat."

Ben looked at DeeNee and shrugged. "This gown has a strange affect on her manners."

"Wedding gowns have a strange affect on women, in general," DeeNee said. "Put stars in their eyes."

Leaning around Sara, Ben checked her vision. She glared at him. "Not a solitary twinkle." He straightened and returned his attention to the thousand and one buttons. "I hope you brought her something to wear that will put a smile on her lips. She's becoming a trifle surly."

"As a matter of fact..."

DeeNee's voice trailed into a sheepish silence and Ben felt Sara stiffen as she turned her head to look at the other woman. "You *did* bring a dress for me." She tried to make it a confident statement, but her tone ended with a slightly shaky question mark. "I noticed you didn't bring it in with you, but I thought you'd left it in your car. You did, didn't you?"

"I didn't." DeeNee raised her shoulders in apology. "I thought it was a joke. Really. You said you accidentally put on a wedding dress and it just didn't occur to me that you had actually put on a wedding dress."

Ben felt Sara's sigh ripple down her back. "Do you want me to button you up again?" he asked.

"No. I want you to unbutton me again and this time, don't stop until you see my underwear."

"I'm here to serve." His fingers returned to the dress with a new energy.

"Do you want to wear this dress?" DeeNee offered.

Ben looked over Sara's shoulder at DeeNee, recognizing in a glance the designer quality and total lack of fashion sense in her outfit. And he knew Sara recognized it, as well.

"Thanks, DeeNee, but then you wouldn't have anything to wear."

"I'll put on the bridal gown."

"Oh, no," Sara said firmly. "Stay away from this dress. It has been trouble from the moment I set eyes on it. Under no circumstances should you go near this wedding gown."

"Well, if you feel that strongly about it, what are you doing in it?" DeeNee asked.

"Trying to get out of it," Sara replied. "Which is no easy task."

"I can see that." DeeNee smiled at Ben. "It must be awful to have an attractive, eligible man unbuttoning your dress."

He smiled back.

"This has been the worst day of my life." Sara put her hands at her waist to hold the dress together as Ben worked his way down. "And how do you know he's eligible?"

DeeNee slid off the bed and slipped on her cloggy-heeled shoes. "No self-respecting wife would let him go out in that shirt and those pants."

"My pants are offended."

"They shouldn't be. It's the shirt I object to. If it was up to me, I'd have you tend bar wearing just the bow tie. It makes the outfit."

Ben preened the points of the D'Lur original. "Arthur loaned it to me. Think I should swipe it?"

"Don't say things like that." Sara's hair swung across her shoulders as she turned her head to give him a one-sided frown. "At Your Service employees do not *swipe* ties or anything else. One incident could cost me my business."

"Geez, Louise, Sara. Don't work yourself into a snit." DeeNee reached over and patted her hand. "It was just a joke."

"Uh-huh, and a bad one. He can say whatever he wants, but not on my time." The auburn hair made another swing across her shoulders, signaling frustration from one gleaming strand to another. "Are you about finished?"

Ben dropped his hands. "I've taken you right down to the bare essentials."

Sara whisked around to splash him with a hurried smile. "Thank you, Ben."

"My pleasure." He had a nice view of her exposed backside in the mirror, and admiring it went a long way toward mitigating any irritation her snappish tone had aroused. "I'm considering becoming a permanent employee. Where else am I going to get paid for unbuttoning women's dresses?"

DeeNee sighed wistfully. "And here I am without a button anywhere on me."

Sara didn't comment about bad jokes this time. Mainly, Ben decided, because she wasn't listening to their nonsensical conversation. She was heading for Arthur's closet, purpose in every step, the open back of the wedding gown gaping to the ribboned lace that rode low on her sexy little hips. After opening the closet door, she stood looking in, her lips pursed, her foot tapping. Ben could tell exactly how fast, too, by the tight jiggle just below her panty line. "I wonder if Arthur has another of those D'Lur ties," she said, obviously not addressing anyone but herself.

"What a great idea." DeeNee voiced the thought Ben couldn't. "You can attend West's party wearing nothing but a bow tie. That would certainly keep things lively."

"I, certainly, would be lively." Ben watched Sara step into the closet and wished he could step right in behind her...and close the door...and take her in his arms.... "So far, this looks like a dull bunch."

"Wait," DeeNee said. "It will get worse, believe me. Once this group of lawyers starts drinking wine, the evening is doomed. You've never heard such a melancholy bunch in your life. I wouldn't even be here if Sara hadn't promised things would be different tonight.''

"I did not promise that." Sara's voice echoed from inside the closet. "And I adore being around this group. They're all fascinating."

DeeNee looked at Ben and shook her head. "She's been buttoned so tightly in that dress, it's squeezed out her sense of humor. Trust me, the evening will go from dull to catatonic, wine or no wine."

"Somehow, I don't think so," Ben whispered, his eyes on Sara as she came out of the closet, measuring one of Arthur's crisp, white shirts against her.

Chapter Six

"How are you doing?" Sara slid in beside Ben at the portable bar and reached past him to remove an empty wine bottle. "Gotten any tips?"

"I've been advised to find another line of work, if that counts." Ben wiped off the counter for probably the fiftieth time and admired her grace and composure for at least the hundredth. She was wearing Arthur's shirt, the tails of which struck her just above mid-thigh and somewhat higher on either side. The jaunty, black-and-white checked bow tie at her neck was not an original work of art, but the slim, solid black bow ties she had fastened around each arm to push up the sleeves were masterpieces of ingenuity. If her black patent heels had been half an inch higher, or the tailored shirt half an inch shorter, or her legs not quite so long and lovely, the whole outfit could have been risqué. But Sara looked like a million dollars, and Ben was as fascinated by her sense of style as by the sheer pluck it took for her to wear such an outfit to a party of blue-serge-suited lawyers. "Can I fix something for you?" he asked.

"Nothing, thanks. I need to keep on my toes. You wouldn't believe the propositions I've gotten this evening."

"No." He drew the word out in disbelief. "Some guy made a pass at the host's fiancée?"

"I am not his fiancée." She looked across the room, smiled when she noticed that West was watching her and lifted her hand in acknowledgment. "Yet."

"Did he make any comment on your new outfit?"

"He said I look incredible."

Incredible was an understatement, but Ben figured he didn't need to say so. "That's it?"

Her eyebrows lifted. "He's a gentleman. Even if he didn't like what I chose to wear, he'd never be anything but complimentary."

Ben had seen that he's-so-wonderful look once too often in the past hour and a half. West Ridgeman might have inherited looks, fortune and connections from his family, but so far he hadn't displayed any qualities that deserved Sara's homage. "Wipe that sappy smile off your face," he advised her. "You look like my aunt Edwynna."

"I beg your pardon?"

"Great-Aunt Edwynna. She used to smile just like that before she grabbed me by the arms and bussed me on both cheeks. It didn't take long before I had other plans whenever she paid a visit."

"And I remind you of her." Sara's forehead wrinkled with a frown. "Is there a point to this story?"

"I am simply making the observation that if you keep smiling at Ridgeman like a bird eyeing a worm, sooner or later he's going to have other plans." He opened a beer and tipped it to his lips for a swallow, enjoying the mix of frustration and thoughts that chased each other across her expressive face.

"I do not look like a bird," she said. "And he doesn't look like a...put that down." She frowned and looked pointedly at the bottle in his hand. "This isn't your party. That isn't your beer. At Your Service employees do not drink on the job."

He set the beer on the counter and pushed it to one side. "What if they're thirsty?"

"Be thirsty on your own time. Tonight you're working for me."

"Then if you fire me, I can finish the beer."

"Forget it. You're mine until midnight."

"I won't last that long if I have to watch you moon around with that sappy smile on your face. You're wasting your time with Ridgeman, you know."

She reached across the bar that separated them and snatched the beer bottle. "That really is none of your business." Turning a cool shoulder to his concern, she headed for the kitchen, and he watched the white cotton shirt clip brusquely against her thighs.

"She's got a killer walk, doesn't she?"

He drew his gaze from the sassy kick of the shirttails to the pin-striped perfection of West Ridgeman, whose lips curved with an abundance of smug. "I like her smile," Ben said. "What can I get for you?"

Ridgeman ignored the offer as he reached around and under the bar to retrieve his own private wine bottle. The cabernet ran into his glass like a stream of red moonlight, as if it, like everything else in the house, was eager to please him. He corked the bottle and put it under the counter. "You're not the guy she normally brings along to tend bar."

"No, I'm better-looking."

"At least you have good taste in ties. That's a D'Lur, if I'm not mistaken."

Ben flicked an imaginary bit of lint off the tie. "Could be. I was in a hurry and grabbed the first thing I found in the closet."

"Really?" Ridgeman lifted his glass. "Where did Sara find you?"

"The yellow pages, under V for versatile. Where did she find you?"

The all-American eyebrows rose a mere hairsbreadth before a well-bred laugh concealed any hint of irritation. "I won her."

"Like a door prize?"

"In a raffle."

"Oh, like a turkey."

Ridgeman sipped his wine. "It was amusing, really. My secretary filled out a raffle ticket in my name, and I won four hours of service from At Your Service. I gave Sara carte blanche to find a present for my sister's birthday, and she came back with a pug, which is an ugly, noisy little dog, but DeeNee declared it the best present I ever gave her. I took Sara out for lunch as a way of expressing my appreciation, and our mutually beneficial relationship was born."

Ben gave her a mental pat on the back for originality and polished the counter again. "You won her in a raffle." He shook his head. "Some guys have all the luck, huh?"

"What can I say?" Ridgeman shrugged without modesty and raised his wineglass in a salute. "It's good to be me."

Watching him walk away from the bar, Ben made another half-hearted swipe of the wet towel over the counter and wondered what Sara saw in the guy. Take away the ego and silver-spoon manners, and he'd be just like any other boring guy with good looks, a good education and a good job in the family firm. So, okay, she knew what she wanted and had the tenacity to go after it. There was nothing wrong with that. He admired her for it, in fact. But he didn't have to endorse her plan. And he didn't have to like it.

He heard the airy slap of the kitchen door as it swung open, then closed, and renewed his needless effort to appear industrious by wiping down the bar.

"This is the last one." Sara set a wine bottle on the counter. "When it's empty, you'll have to push the soft drinks."

"A gentleman like Ridgeman is bound to have a few extra bottles stashed somewhere."

"He only buys this brand for entertaining. He says this particular wine is a waste of good grapes, but apparently most of the guests don't share that opinion."

"Taste is a personal choice." Ben took the neutral, nonpartisan position. Otherwise, Sara might take away his bar towel, and he'd have to find another way to look busy. "Some people prefer to drink red wine and some prefer to drink white and some people don't like wine no matter what shade it comes in."

"You, for instance, prefer beer."

"Not at all. I often drink plain water." He gave her his best smile, trying to coax a similar response from her, but she had an iron will. "Your boyfriend was just here for a refill. He said he won you with a raffle ticket, which is either an amazing bit of luck for him or a brilliant marketing strategy by you.''

''I am rather proud of that idea.''

''How many tickets were in the final drawing?''

''Trade secret.''

''So you snared Mr. Wonderful with the old raffle-ticket ploy. Very clever. Wouldn't have worked if you'd been ten years older and unattractive.'' He smiled. ''In my opinion, of course.''

This time she smiled back. ''Luckily, I didn't ask for your opinion.'' Turning, she scanned the crowd. ''Have you seen DeeNee since she came downstairs?''

''No, can't say I have. She probably knows what cheap wine her brother serves his guests and is huddled up somewhere with the cooking sherry.''

''The wine isn't cheap,'' Sara corrected in an automatic tone. ''Merely not absurdly expensive.''

Blindly infatuated, Ben thought. And she hadn't tasted the wine, either. ''So is DeeNee still here?''

''I guess so. Her car is parked by the van, at any rate, and Annette said she was in the kitchen a little while ago. DeeNee is a very fine cook. In case you didn't know, she prepared all the hors d'oeuvres for tonight. You should try one.''

''I'm not allowed to eat on the job. My employer's real hard-nosed about it.''

Her brown eyes skimmed to his, and her lips curved in a provocative line. ''You do catch on quick... and I do appreciate that in a man.''

''Yes, well, you'll never convince me that Ridgeman's a quick study.''

''He doesn't need to be. He was born knowing more than most men ever learn.''

Something about that *most men* sounded rather personal. "Do you make snap judgments about everyone you meet or only men you find physically attractive?"

"Meaning you, I suppose?"

"Meaning me. You know how quickly I catch on."

"Then you shouldn't have any difficulty understanding this." A challenge sparkled in her eyes as she turned her back on him and sashayed across the room. Ridgeman looked up and smiled at her approach, then moved forward to cup her elbow in his hand and guide her into his conversational circle.

Ben wished she hadn't carried off his beer.

"Quick, pour me a drink and pretend you find me fascinating."

Turning his head, he encountered the feisty blue eyes of DeeNee Ridgeman. She was standing next to the bar, darting glances at a particular cluster of dark-suited lawyers. He leaned toward her. "Do I have to pretend or can I actually find you fascinating?"

Her attention swung to him. "I have to tell you, Ben, you have a better line than the guy Sara usually brings."

"I'm glad to hear it. None of the guests have lingered long enough to hear my line. I was beginning to think I must be the dullest bartender ever to wipe down this counter."

"Better to be dull than invisible." She sighed and looked longingly at the legal conclave once more. "Pour me a shot of bottled water, and we'll be dull and invisible together."

Ben unscrewed a bottle cap and drowned an ice cube in sparkling water before handing the glass to her. "I made it a double," he said. "You look like you need it."

She wrinkled her nose and swallowed half the water in a single draw. "Have you ever been in love with the wrong person, Ben?"

"Are you kidding? Every single time. I've never been in love with the right person, or I suppose I would have stopped looking then and there. What about you?"

"This is the first time for me." She swirled the water in the glass and watched it go around and around.

"To be in love?" he asked.

"To be in love with the wrong person. Actually, he's the right person. That's why it's so wrong."

"Is he married?"

"Worse. He has principles."

"Oh, no. A fatal attraction."

"Yes, well, it might be, if he could ever stop looking through me and notice that I'm not only visible, but could be his for the asking." Plunking the glass on the bar, she splashed the counter with her futility. "Hit me again...but this time give me some of my brother's private stash of cabernet. Pour yourself some, too."

"I've been informed that I'm on duty."

"Well, it's just become your duty to entertain me. I'll accept the responsibility and tell Sara I forced you to have a drink."

"Somehow I don't think that will mean much to her." He looked across the room, watched her move among the guests as if she'd been born for the part. "On the other hand, she doesn't seem very interested in me."

"See, there's a perfect example. She thinks she's in love with my brother," DeeNee said.

Ben uncorked the bottle and filled her glass. "I'd say she's pretty well convinced of it."

"He is totally wrong for her, you know. I wish she had worn the wedding dress to the party. That would have scared West right out of his Bostonians."

"Are you against the idea of having Sara in the family?"

"Of course not. I'd adore having her as a sister."

"But?" Ben posed the unspoken objection.

"As a brother, West isn't so bad, but he won't be a good husband. At least not for Sara. He'll change her into a wife fit for a Ridgeman and make her unhappy into the bargain." She shrugged. "Just my opinion, though. And what do I know? I'm invisible to the one man I could make ecstatically happy. Go figure, huh?"

Ben liked her. If Ridgeman had inherited the better portion of the family looks and luck, his sister had been gifted with wry humor and a good heart. He looked at the group of men she kept eyeing. "Which one is he?"

Her eyes widened in assumed innocence. "Who?"

"The guy who doesn't know what he's missing."

She sized Ben up with an artful glance. "Am I that obvious?"

"Well, I'm standing pretty close."

Resting her hip against the bar, she wrinkled her nose then sipped the wine. "He's standing by the terrace doors. His name is Harry Schaffer. He's short, balding at thirty, intellectual and terribly sexy. You know the type. An abbreviated Paul Newman without much hair.''

''I see him. Is he going to notice that I find you fascinating?''

''Probably not, but don't let that stop you.''

''That could be the solution, you know. Nothing attracts a man's attention faster than seeing a woman flirting with another man.''

''First, he'd have to be able to *see* me.''

''I find it hard to believe you don't know how to arrange that.''

''Maybe I do.'' She looked at Ben thoughtfully. ''You'll help me, right?''

''I am at your service, Miss Ridgeman.''

She had a little girl's laugh, and he couldn't help but respond to it.

From the corner of his eye, he caught the silky movement of Sara's hair as she looked his way. Even from across the room, he could tell she was curious. At Your Service employees probably weren't allowed to laugh while on duty, either. A moment later, Ridgeman's gaze followed hers to the bar and narrowed slightly before he bent his head and said something to Sara.

''Uh-oh.'' DeeNee's voice dropped to a confiding level. ''Big Brother is watching us. He'll be over here in a minute with some dumb excuse to drag me away. The truth is, he's such a snob and he can't understand what he calls my strange compulsion to fraternize with the hired help. It drives him crazy.''

''Hmm.'' Ben kept his eye on Sara, who was keeping an eye on him. ''I would have thought he'd understand perfectly.''

"Not West. Sara's the only woman he's ever dated who is gainfully employed. He's very impressed because she has her own business."

"I figured he was very impressed with the way her hips move when she walks."

"That, too," DeeNee agreed.

Sara touched West's sleeve, smiled at him, then walked toward the bar. Ben was as impressed as hell—and he couldn't even see her backside.

"Well, our fun is over for the moment." DeeNee set her glass on the counter. "Sara thinks it's sweet that West worries about me. She told me once she wished she had a protective older brother." DeeNee shook her head. "Ignorance is bliss, I guess. Hi, Sara. Don't scold Ben. I insisted he have a drink with me."

Sara answered with a self-assured smile. "I'm sure he told you that would go against company policy."

"I did. And you'll notice I do not have a beverage in my hand or tucked out of sight beneath the counter." Ben held her gaze with a rich and warm amusement. "That's because I'm a quick study."

"I like him a thousand times better than that frilled shirt you usually bring." DeeNee reached over and patted Ben's cheek. "And he's so very helpful."

"Just doing my duty."

"Yes, well, let's not go overboard with that duty stuff." Sara glanced restlessly at West.

DeeNee sighed dramatically. "Okay, okay. I'll move on before my brother brings out the chastity belt. But, Ben, I'm counting on you for later."

"I'm already looking forward to it." He gave her an encouraging wink and she blew him a kiss.

Sara turned to him the moment DeeNee was out of earshot. "Did you make a *date* with her?"

Ben raised his eyebrows. "Is dating against company policy, too?"

"Look, I know this is the first time you've been exposed to this kind of upscale situation, but you are here in a professional capacity only. Flirting with DeeNee is inappropriate."

"You're flirting with her brother."

"I am not flirting, and it isn't the same thing at all. West and I are . . . friends."

He wiped the towel across the counter. "I see. It's all right for you to bat your eyes at Mr. Raffle Ticket, but not for me to talk to his sister. Is that what you're saying?"

Her eyes flashed with an attractive annoyance. "This isn't open for discussion. I hired you for the evening, and that means I set the standards."

"One standard for you and another for your employees. Well, let me get something off my chest, Ms. At Your Service." He reached up, unfastened the middle button of his shirt and paused before undoing a second.

Her eyes widened. "What do you think you're doing?"

"Making sure I have your attention." He kept his hand on the shirt placket as he leaned toward her. "If there *was* any flirting going on here—and I'm not saying there was or there wasn't—it isn't any of your business. And for the record, she approached me."

"Of course, she did. You're the bartender. Now, button your shirt."

He ignored the interruption. "I like DeeNee. She's sweet and funny, and if I did ask her for a date, it would be because I like sweet and funny women, not for any other reason."

"Are you implying I have some mysterious ulterior motive for flirting with West?"

"See there? You admit you were flirting."

"I admit nothing. You're the one who started this." She glanced self-consciously over her shoulder, making sure no one else was paying any attention. "Please, Ben, button your shirt."

He did, wondering if he could have provoked her into threatening to do it for him. "There's no need to get defensive, Sara. I'm not saying there's anything wrong with flirting. It keeps life interesting."

"Well, while you're working for me, keep your shirt buttoned, your interests to yourself and your seductive green eyes off West's sister."

"See, that's something else we have in common. I think your eyes are seductive, too."

The startled look of awareness that flared momentarily in her sexy brown eyes was worth the effort. Her voice betrayed none of it, however. "You and I have nothing in common."

"Of course we do. We both know what we want and we go after it, no holds barred." He smiled, daring her to deny it. "If you want Ridgeman, he might as well raise the white flag right now and be done with it."

"And I suppose you believe you could wrap DeeNee around your little finger with no trouble at all."

"Oh, I wouldn't say it would be no trouble." His hand brushed the length of her arm as he wiped a minuscule watermark from the bar, and he smiled to himself when she moved out of reach. "She wouldn't be the challenge you are, of course, but with a woman, there's always some trouble involved."

"You're out of your league here, Ben."

He laughed softly. "In your opinion."

"In point of fact. There isn't a woman in this room who would succumb to your charms for more than half an hour."

He pursed his lips, more than a little annoyed by her attitude. "That almost sounds like a dare."

Sara crossed her arms at her waist, then apparently realized how defensive she must look and dropped them to her sides. "If I felt the need to challenge you, I wouldn't leave any doubt as to my intention."

He lifted the glass set aside for gratuities and held it out to her, spilling its emptiness all around. "Maybe you should leave a tip, instead. I'm not sure I can be bought off, but it might be worth a try."

"What a time to be penniless." She gave a coy, less-than-regretful shrug. "I'm afraid I have nothing to give you...except advice."

"Here. I've got fifty cents." He pulled two quarters from his pocket and dropped them into the glass. "We'll consider it a loan."

"Consider it whatever you like. Just remember you're here to tend bar, not to socialize with the guests." She turned on a dime and then abruptly turned back. "And for the record, there is nothing wrong with knowing the qualities I want in a mate. The size of his bank account is not important, but ambition and drive certainly are."

"What about companionship? Love? Back rubs?"

Her lips snapped into a practiced smile as a man and a woman approached the bar. Ben filled their orders with self-assured good humor. "The tips are lousy here," he said after the couple had walked away without so much as a thank-you, much less a glance at the two quarters in the glass. "No wonder you said I could keep them."

"Perhaps service is the problem."

His eyebrows went up. "Knocking the employees is not good for morale, boss. But don't worry, I know you didn't mean it. You're just upset because I'm having more fun than you are."

"I am not upset, and *fun* has nothing to do with it."

"My point, exactly. You're not having fun and I am. It's unfair, I know, but then, I didn't set the standards."

Irritation lined the set of her lips. "I knew I'd be sorry I didn't check your references."

"It was fate. You bowled me over with your charm…so to speak. Of course, if I'd spent more than a half hour with you, I might not have succumbed . . . so to speak."

"You succumbed to the offer of a paycheck," she said snippily. "Let's not confuse the issue with charm."

Ben wished he wasn't so competitive—or so susceptible to women with attitudes, or so intrigued by this particular and inconsistent redhead. "I have a proposition for you, Sara. A small wager."

She glanced over her shoulder again to make sure no one was watching before she leaned close to Ben. "Let me guess. You're going to try to get me to bet that you can't seduce me. I am not stupid. I know where this is leading.''

"You jump to conclusions faster than anyone I've ever met—with the possible exception of my father. He believes he's invulnerable, too. However, contrary to your unflattering and erroneous opinion of me, I do have principles, and I would never seduce a woman just to prove a point.''

"I can't wait to hear the rest of this.''

He almost backed off at that point, but the sheer energy she exuded, the zest she exhibited in every action, dragged him ever deeper into this ill-advised flirtation. "I will wager my paycheck that before the last stroke of midnight, I can charm at least one woman in this room into spending more than a half hour in my company—and kiss her into the bargain.''

"That would fall under the category of seduction—which is against your principles—or flirtation, which is against mine.''

"I did not say seduction is against my principles. I said I wouldn't do it just to prove a point.''

She cocked an eyebrow. "And the difference is?''

"I would be happy to demonstrate.''

"Oh, I'll just bet you would.''

"Good. Double or nothing?''

She shook her head. "You know, Ben, you really deserve to be taken down a notch or two.''

"Don't tell me. You believe you're just the woman to do it.''

"If I wanted to, I could.'' Smug confidence shadowed her smile. "Without half trying.''

"You're very confident . . . even for a redhead.''

"Sara?" West's hand cupped her elbow. "Is there a problem?"

"No, not at all. Ben and I were just discussing professional etiquette."

"Good. There's someone I would like you to meet, if you can drag yourself away from instructing the bartender for a moment or two."

"Of course." She glanced at Ben, her confidence veiled by the same polite facade that marked every other guest in the room. "We were finished with our conversation."

"I thought you were." West guided her in a smooth turn, never once acknowledging Ben's presence by so much as a direct glance. "There's an old family friend who—"

"Sara." Ben interrupted, reclaiming her attention. "Thanks for the tip."

For an instant, the confidence returned to center stage in her eyes, and her smile challenged and captivated him all over again. "Think nothing of it," she said. "I wouldn't want you to go home empty-handed."

"As I was saying..." West turned her like a pancake, and Ben was awarded a view of her back, which wasn't altogether a bad thing because she was poetry in motion. He watched the sway of her hips with unabashed admiration and thought that if Ridgeman was half as smart as he thought he was, he'd find a way to walk several steps behind her.

There was a dim rumble in the kitchen, a noise that grew louder and more distracting, until everyone in the room heard and turned to look at the door. Into the momentary hush, a clatter of metal fell like a gunshot and then a voice lifted out of the noise like a phoenix. "Hey, get out of there! Leave that alone! Drop it! Drop it, I tell you!" Another clatter, and the swinging door slammed back on its hinges as Cleo dashed into the room, carrying a slab of roast beef nearly as big as her head and followed by a squat, tan-and-black dog with a crumpled nose and the gleam of fresh meat in its beady eyes. Behind them, Arthur gave chase, a carving knife in one hand, a cutting board in the other.

"Brody!" DeeNee stepped into the dogs' path.

"Cleo!" Sara stepped in front of DeeNee.

"You *know* this dog?" West didn't step in front of anyone. He just looked astonished.

Ben didn't step up to claim responsibility. As the dogs veered in his direction, he jumped from behind the bar, sending it in an unfortunate and unerring collision with a pedestal table and a rather ugly piece of sculpture. Bottles crashed, beer spewed, wine gushed, liquor poured, and the artwork shattered, lost to the world forever in a sea of booze. Worse, Cleo was too agile for him, and Ben caught only the end of her tail. He tried to hold her, but she slipped free and raced for the open terrace doors with her prize.

Quick-thinking Harry and his colleagues blocked her exit, although Ben wasn't sure why. Maybe they thought the roast beef was worth saving even if the reception was now beyond repair. Like an oil spill, Cleo covered the room in a matter of seconds, leaving devastation in her wake. A glass-topped table tipped over and broke apart as she tried to squeeze under it. She hurdled a sofa and landed, none too delicately, on the terrazzo tile. Her feet slipped on the polished floor, and her hind legs went into a skid that wiped out a tray of hors d'oeuvres and several glasses. Behind her, the pug grabbed bits of fallen hors d'oeuvres as he scurried to keep up. Wherever Cleo had jumped or skirted a piece of furniture, Brody left his footprints, tracking wine across the sofa, two Oriental rugs and a white cashmere afghan.

One woman of matronly stature stepped onto the seat cushion of a wing chair and jumped up and down as she yelled, "Mad dogs! Mad dogs!"

Far from being mad, the two dogs seemed pretty sane as they maneuvered past would-be dogcatchers and startled guests to race up the stairs. Ben would have caught Cleo if he hadn't noticed that the mad-dog matron was about to tip over in her chair and stopped to prevent the disaster. When he reached the foyer, Sara, DeeNee, West and Arthur were standing at the foot of the curving stairway looking up at the two dogs as they gobbled their prize on the second-floor landing.

"What idiot let that dog in here?" Ridgeman's voice trembled with outrage.

"She must have come in with Brody," DeeNee said. "Through the doggy door."

"That fat little pug can barely squeeze through there, much less a dog as big as that one."

"The terrace doors are open off the living room." Ben pointed out the logical explanation. "The dogs could have come in any time and found their way to the kitchen."

Ridgeman wasn't ready for logic. "When I find out who owns that black disaster, they're going to find themselves facing a court date and a lawsuit for damages."

Ben didn't like threats, and he certainly didn't like them from lawyers. "Then I suppose you're looking for—"

"Me." Sara stepped in front of West, effectively preventing Ben from doing so. "I'll accept full responsibility. Cleo came with me."

Chapter Seven

From inside the van, Sara stared morosely at the big house. "West will never speak to me again."

"Or me." Ben turned in his seat to look in the back, where Cleo lay in abject humiliation. "And that goes triple for you, hellhound."

"Don't call her that." Sara rested her head against the seat back. "She's more miserable than I am."

"She deserves to have a world-class stomachache. She all but swallowed that piece of beef whole."

"Brody ate part of it."

"One bite to three of her gulps. I'm just grateful she didn't throw up until I got her outside."

"A disastrous night," Sara said. "Although I don't know why I'm surprised. Murphy's Law has nothing on the Gunnerson Rule of Thumb."

"Which is?"

"When opportunity knocks, take cover."

Ben laughed and reached behind his seat. "I filched these from the bar." He held up two beer bottles. "I'm sure you have a rule of one sort or another against At Your Service employees pilfering alcoholic beverages while on duty. But when the bar crashed, I figured I was out of a job, anyway.'' He offered her one of the bottles. ''It isn't the private stock, but it isn't the cheap stuff, either.''

She ought to hang tough and refuse to partake of ill-gotten goods. On the other hand, she was out of a job, too... more or less. The referrals she'd hoped to gain among West's associates had crashed with the party, and by the time she reimbursed West for all the damage, the cost of a couple of beers would be small potatoes. ''Did you steal a bottle opener, too?''

''Real men are born with all the tools they need.'' He wedged off the cap with his thumb and handed the bottle to her. ''Bottoms up.''

''Aren't you having one?'' she asked. ''After you went to all the trouble of smuggling them out of the house?''

With a slight smile, he shoved his thumb against the second bottle cap and flipped it across the dashboard.

As she raised the bottle to her lips, Sara noticed the furtive way he pressed his thumb against his mouth. ''You didn't hurt your tool, did you?''

A sheepish glint merely enhanced the seductive humor in his eyes. ''I think from now on I'll carry a bottle opener in my pocket.''

''Don't be too hasty. That kind of macho muscle flexing impresses a lot of women. DeeNee, for one.''

Ben took a swallow of beer. ''Nope. She prefers the shy, intellectual type.''

''Uh-huh. That goes to show how much you know about women like DeeNee Ridgeman.''

''Oh, I suspect I know her a little better than you think I do.''

"After talking to her for what? Ten minutes? Fifteen at the most?"

"I could tell everything I needed to know by the way she blinked her eyes."

"She must have blinked in Morse code, then."

He shifted in the seat, leaned against the door and propped his arm on the steering wheel. When his lips formed a sensual curve of challenge, the van suddenly seemed small and far too intimate. "You aren't the only person in the world who can rely on intuition, Sara. I'll pit my abilities against yours any time you say."

She liked his self-assurance, even if he was overconfident. "You're not going to trap me into betting against you, Ben. I'm on to your tricks. Besides, even if you're right about DeeNee, you're not her type, so it doesn't matter, either way."

"You're saying I'm not a shy, intellectual male?"

"You're not shy, that's for sure."

"I could be if I tried."

"Why would you try to be something you're not?"

"Good question."

His expression made her uncomfortable somehow, and she rubbed the back of her neck. "Let's leave. Everyone is gone. We've done all the cleanup and counted all the silverware. I, for one, am ready to close the books on this disaster."

"I'm afraid we can't go anywhere just yet."

"The dog has the keys again," she said with a sigh.

"No, I have the keys. The dog is too embarrassed to lift her head, much less play any more games."

"Well, even if I forgot something, it will still be here tomorrow, and I can..." An unsettling realization flashed across her brain, and she squeezed her eyes shut in the vain hope of blocking it out. "The wedding dress is still under Arthur's bed."

"I'm glad you remember where you left it, because we're going to have to go back for it."

"I think I'd rather enter the witness-protection program and forget I'd ever seen that dress."

"Not an option. For better or worse, I'm responsible for that dress until it's delivered to its final destination. And for best or worst, that dress is your responsibility until it's safely in my hands. So just go up there, knock on the back door and ask Arthur to give it back."

Sara did not want to get within ten feet of the house or Arthur, much less the wedding dress. "Why don't I wait here while you do it."

"Arthur isn't going to give me anything but a hard time. Go on. He likes you."

"Oh, right. He practically caught my backside in the door when he closed it behind me. He isn't going to give either one of us the time of day, especially not at this hour."

Ben glanced at his watch. "Maybe you could ask West to get the dress and give it to us."

She cringed at the thought. "I can't face him. Not this soon after... Well, I can't. Besides, I can't think of any reasonable way to explain how that wedding gown got under Arthur's bed."

"Then I'd say we have something of a dilemma on our hands."

"We could come back tomorrow and get it."

"I should be halfway to California by then."

Pursing her lips in a frown, Sara stared at the house. "We might be able to sneak in and out without either one of them knowing."

"Ah, a plan is forming."

"Not much of one. It would involve some climbing."

Ben followed her gaze to the second story. "The trellis?"

"If you have a better idea, I'd love to hear it."

"You're completely opposed to knocking on the door?"

"Completely. You're positive this can't wait until tomorrow?"

"Positive."

She looked at the trellis again. "I must be out of my mind."

BEN LACED HIS fingers to form a cup as he bent down. "Put your foot in here and I'll give you a boost."

"You're sure this trellis will hold me?"

"If it doesn't, you won't have far to fall."

"And you'll be here to catch me, right?"

"Of course."

"If you need to climb up first, in order to prove your masculinity, I'll step down and let you go ahead."

"Thanks for the offer, but I couldn't strip you of the opportunity to prove the equality of the sexes. Now, give me your foot."

"Okay, okay." Setting her bare right foot in his palm, Sara reached for a handhold in the lattice and prayed it was strong enough to hold her. He lifted her and held her steady as she gained her balance, then boosted her up. The trellis shook with her weight, but nothing broke, so she pulled herself up, climbing a little higher and acquiring a little more confidence with each new foothold. Ben's steadying hand slipped from her back to her waist to her hips, and a shiver rocketed up her spine, nearly costing her the footage she'd gained and making the trellis quiver with her sudden weak-in-the-knees response.

"Be careful," he whispered.

Good advice. Ben Northcross was not a part of her plans, no matter how strong an attraction he evoked. And if she wasn't clinging to a few insubstantial strips of wood, she might confront the issue with him here and now, just so they'd both know where they stood. Instead, she scrambled up to the second story like a long-legged spider. She gripped the balcony rail with one hand and swung one foot up to search for leverage. A sudden resistance tightened across her shoulders and grew stronger as she moved against it. "Something's wrong." Hanging like a sloth from a tree branch, she tried to look down to see the problem.

"You're stuck."

"No kidding."

"I think your shirt is caught on a nail, but it's hard to tell in the dark."

"Great. Should I climb down?"

"Can you?"

"Of course—" she moved her foot off the balcony and searched for a toehold, but the shirt pulled taut around her neck, nearly choking her, and she resumed the sloth position. "Not. Now what do we do?"

"Hold on. I'm coming up."

Dudley Do-Right to save the day, she thought. Although at the moment, she was particularly grateful. It would be very embarrassing to have West discover her in the morning dangling from his trellis like an overdressed praying mantis—and she did not want any more embarrassing moments. The wood quivered beneath her, and for a split second she had the silly thought that even wood was receptive to the touch of Ben's hands. But it was his movements that made the whole thing shake, his weight added to hers that caused the ominous snap of a board. "Be careful," she said.

"I'm doing my damnedest." His voice tensed on the last word as another board creaked beneath his boots. The pull on her shoulders increased, and a moment later his hand slipped beneath the tented fabric and splayed supportively across her lower back. "Lean on me and ease your grip on the railing," he said. "But don't let go."

"Don't worry. An earthquake couldn't move me at this point." But as a scintillating warmth spread from the center of his palm across her back, she shifted. The warmth spiraled in new circles, like ripples on a pond, surrounding an empty place inside her. This had to stop, she decided, and got a tighter grip on the balcony rail. But as she arched her back away from his touch, the sensation moved to his fingertips and imprinted on her skin, leaving five points of rebuttal, five heated spots of awareness.

"You're going the wrong way, Sara. Relax and let me brace you with my hand."

Two opposing actions, in her opinion. To relax, she should move away from his touch. To get loose, she should move closer. When she weighed in the embarrassment factor, getting loose won hands down. Taking a deep breath, she released her death grip on the railing until she felt the smooth, strong support of his touch. Awareness fluttered down her spine in a delicate spiral, and she shivered.

"Be still," he said. "I'm going to tear this loose."

She stayed still through the sound of ripping cotton and lectured her body on misleading her brain. Just as the resistance on her shoulders eased, she heard another board crack. "We'd better get off this," she said, and pulled herself up and onto the balcony.

Several splintering noises later, Ben swung up beside her. "We're going to have to find another way down."

Sara stepped away from him to look over the rail at the sagging trellis. "I guess I'll add lattice repairs to my list of damages."

"May as well add a new shirt for Arthur, too." Ben smoothed the tails one over the other, without touching her, but evoking a startling awareness all the same. "This one is torn from... Well, you could catch pneumonia."

"At this point, pneumonia sounds almost appealing." She shook her head at the dilemma facing her. "If West finds out I'm the one responsible for this, too..."

"You're going to marry him. He'll forgive you before the ceremony."

"As if there's much chance for a proposal now. He was really angry."

"I don't see why. The party was dull as dirt until the Brody and Cleo Show." Ben tried the window. "This is locked. Is there an alarm?"

"No."

"No? You're sure?"

"No alarm," she stated firmly. "What are you going to do?"

"Break the glass."

"Are you nuts? That would be breaking and entering. We could be arrested." She looked around for a solution. "We'll just have to get down from here somehow and figure out another way to get the dress."

He jiggled the window. "Here's a thought. You find a way down, get a ladder and rescue me."

"There's no point in getting snippy. This was as much your idea as mine."

"It wasn't my idea for you to put on the wedding gown."

"It wasn't my idea, either...exactly." She still couldn't explain what had come over her, why the dress had fascinated her so. "And there really isn't any point in our arguing about it. You'll get paid for your trouble tonight and you'll get paid again when you deliver the dress, so I don't see where you have any grounds for complaint."

He turned toward her. "Money isn't going to solve our immediate problem. Now, what do you want to do? Break the window? Or sit here until someone opens it?"

There had to be another option. She leaned against the rail and looked up, down and to either side. Several feet across and a few feet up was another, larger balcony, dark with shadows and the unknown. A few feet farther on in the same direction the roof slanted into a steep eave over the kitchen door. A few feet to the right of the balcony, the rock facade gave way to a decorative brick wall, which stretched to the corner of the house. Directly overhead, the roof climbed to a precipitous angle over the third floor. Below them— well, jumping didn't seem like an appealing choice from this perspective. Gathering her courage, she took a giant step and levered her body onto the balcony railing, balancing precariously like a tightrope walker. "Stay here," she said. "I'll return to save the day."

BEN NEARLY CHOKED on his surprise, but by the time he reached out to stop her, she had swung her foot to the left and was climbing, finding minute toe and fingerholds in the rock facade. "Come back here, Sara." He made a supreme effort to keep his voice low and level and not give in to the urge to yell at the top of his lungs. "That is not a good idea."

"Ssh! Do you want Arthur to hear you?"

Maybe he ought to alert the butler. Tell him to call an ambulance or the rescue squad. But even as he worried, Sara climbed the wall like a fly and reached the higher balcony. Ben shook his head in grudging and growing admiration before he swung his foot over the railing and climbed after her.

"I WOULD HAVE come around and opened the window for you," she said when he dropped onto the balcony beside her. "Didn't you believe me?"

"It's one thing to let a woman risk her neck while you hold the ladder. It's something else again to wait while she goes to get the ladder to rescue you." He lifted one shoulder in a shrug. "It's a male thing."

"I hope it's a male thing to carry the proper tools." She indicated the French doors. "I'm not sure how much use your thumb will be with that latch."

Ben moved closer to get a better look. "I told you that real men always have the proper tool." He took his billfold from his hip pocket, pulled a piece of plastic from inside and handed it to her. "Here, hold this a minute." He stooped to examine the lock.

"Ooh, a gold card." Sara turned the credit card over in her hands. "Good thing it doesn't have to be current to get us inside."

"What?" He glanced at her.

"Your card. It expired four months ago."

"No, it didn't. You read the date wrong."

She checked. "My mistake. It expired five months ago."

"That can't be right. I probably just forgot to take it out of my wallet when the new card arrived."

"Uh-huh," she said, knowing that in his position, she'd have made the same excuse. "If it's any consolation, mine expired of exposure last Christmas. Against my better judgment, a family member borrowed my card and practically wore the magnetic strip right off. The credit-card company not so kindly decided to put the poor thing out of its misery."

"Your credit or your relative?"

"My credit, unfortunately."

"Was that the same family member who wrecked your van?"

"No. It was my father, the original Peter Pan."

Ben looked at her, and even in the dusky shadows she caught the glimmer of understanding in his expression. *Don't say anything,* she told him silently. *Don't try to make it better. Don't trivialize my anger with some trite comment about loving fathers and family ties.*

He reached for the card and pulled it from her fingers. "Are you sure you want to break into your fiancé's house? It would be a whole lot easier to knock on the door."

Her lips curved with an appreciative smile for all the things he hadn't said. "No, it wouldn't," she answered.

"A minute ago you were worried about breaking and entering. What happened? Did you climb above such principles?"

"I was worried about breaking and entering *noisily.* It stands to reason that the less noise we make, the less the chances we'll get caught. And if we can get in and out without getting caught, then principles won't actually come into play."

"And what if we should get caught?"

"Then I'll tell West the whole story. But this way, there's at least a fifty-fifty chance he won't ever have to know about the wedding dress."

"What about the fifty-fifty chance that you'll have to tell him it's a magic wedding dress?"

"I'm not mentioning that part, either way."

"What a shame. He'd probably be charmed out of his socks."

"Uh-huh. Are you going to be able to get the door open?"

The reply came in a soft, metallic click. Stepping closer to Ben, she waited for him to open the door. He stood, bringing his body into contact with hers, and the sudden tension saturated the shadows with awareness. Sara jerked back awkwardly and obviously. Her heart fluttered like a bird in flight, despite her efforts to calm it with deep breathing. She was just overexcited, that's all. A trifle nervous, which was understandable, considering the risk she was taking. None of it had anything to do with Ben. She simply needed to keep reminding herself of that.

"Did it work?" Her voice quivered and she steadied it. "Can you open the door now?"

"I'm about to try. You're sure there isn't an alarm?"

"I have never seen one, and I've been in the house dozens of times."

"Visiting the downstairs bedroom. I remember."

"You weren't there. Here, let me do the honors." She reached for the latch, closing her hand over his and feeling the tension surround her all over again. Before she could pull her hand back, the door opened and an earsplitting siren demolished the quiet.

"Intuition tells me that's an alarm." He grabbed her hand and jerked her inside. "You might want to polish up those principles you mentioned."

Her heartbeat thudded in her ears, and disaster loomed like Godzilla over Tokyo. "What should we do?" she whispered, despite the loud whooping of the alarm.

"First, I'm locking the door in the faint hope they might believe it's a false alarm. After that, I'm open for suggestions."

As her eyes adjusted to the dim light, Sara got the glimmer of a plan. "This would be an excellent time to follow the Gunnerson Rule of Thumb—"

They looked at each other and finished the sentence in unison. "Take cover!"

"Hear that?" Sara whispered. "The alarm stopped."

Ben stared at the bed slat directly above his head and wondered if this unusual evening was about to be capped off by a trip to jail. "I imagine West or Arthur turned it off."

"Then we're practically home free." Her voice was rich with satisfaction. "West will never even know we were in the house."

"Turning off the alarm isn't exactly an all clear."

She was quiet for a moment or two, but he could almost hear the plans turning in her head. "How long before it's okay to make a move out from under this bed?"

"A long time."

"Have you ever done this before?"

"What? Hidden under a bed? Or broken into a house?" The ensuing quiet made him smile into the darkness.

"Either one." Her whisper echoed with a faint suspicion, and he decided not to tease her further. "I have to confess to hiding under beds as a kid, but breaking and entering is a first for me."

"Me, too."

"Do you think we'll get arrested?"

"Nah."

"Are you scared?"

"No. I've been arrested before. It's not that bad. Are you scared?"

"A little."

The silence filled with the soft, rapid rhythm of her breathing, and he found her hand and enclosed it in his. Her pulse raced beneath the pad of his thumb, and he soothed it with gentling strokes. "You're safe. Just think positive thoughts."

"I can't believe I'm under here."

"That isn't positive. Think about how much better hiding under a bed is than hiding in a closet."

"Only because this carpet is so thick. If this room had hardwood floors, it wouldn't be so great under here."

"I disagree. It isn't what you're lying on that matters. It's who is lying beside you."

He felt her move and knew she had turned her head toward him. "Now that's a profound thought for a deliveryman."

"I told you I was the shy, intellectual type."

"Well, Mr. Intellectual, this must be an entirely new perspective for you."

Ben turned his head to meet her gaze in the soft, close darkness. "I'll admit I generally spend more time on a bed than under it, but I'm open to new experiences."

"You've gotten more experience than you bargained for this time, though, haven't you?"

And then some, Ben thought. "If I had known all the tools I'd need for this job, I'd have asked for a bigger percentage of the tips."

"You get to keep the entire fifty cents already."

"Hey, that's right, and when you pay back the fifty cents I loaned you, I'll have a whole dol—"

"Ssh. Do you hear something?"

"No."

"Well, listen."

He listened. "I don't hear anything," he said finally.

"Neither do I. I thought I heard voices, but I guess not." Her fingers curled into his palm, seeking warmth or shelter, or maybe just the security of a touch. "This day has been like some fractured fairy tale where nothing turns out the way it was supposed to."

"You mean you didn't plan this?"

"I planned to charm the eyebrows off West and his guests. I planned to impress the heck out of everyone and increase my business dramatically. I planned to show West how well I fit in with his friends and how easily I can blend into his life. And then, like a bolt out of the blue, the wedding dress makes an appearance and I wind up sharing the underside of a bed with a stranger."

"You and I haven't been strangers since the moment you crashed into my arms."

"That's true. We *have* been through a lot together in a few short hours, and you've been an awfully good sport about everything."

"Hey, this is the most entertaining evening I've had in years. And I'm always a good sport. See, I told you I'd be more help to you than Cleo would."

"You're right, and I won't mention that she has been absolutely no help at all." Sara's tone dwindled to a discouraged sigh. "Do you think there is even a slight chance that we'll get out of this with some degree of dignity still intact?''

"Dignity is overrated. I'll be happy to escape with the dress."

The door opened abruptly and a light came on, channeling illumination around the three open sides of the bed. Purposeful footsteps crossed the room, and Ben could follow the high-gloss Italian leather of West Ridgeman's shoes. The French doors rattled lightly, and then the shoes disappeared from view.

"What's he doing?" Sara whispered, and Ben squeezed her hand, cautioning her to complete silence.

"Everything seems to be in order, sir." Arthur's voice came from the direction of the doorway, and the shoes reentered the room. "Shall I phone the alarm company?"

"Yes." The French doors closed, and the latch clicked into place. "And ask them to send a technician on Monday to check the wiring. This is the third time in two months that some slight movement of these doors has set off the alarm. It's obviously too sensitive."

"Yes, sir. I'll take care of it."

"Oh, and Arthur?"

"Yes, sir?"

"Call the garage in the morning and have Miss Gunnerson's van towed in for service. It's still parked in back, and I'm certain she wouldn't have left it behind if she'd had any other choice. You might make sure it's locked before you retire, not that any thief in his right mind would steal it."

"I will check on the van, sir. Will there be anything else?"

"No. Good night, Arthur."

"Good night, Mr. West."

The door closed, but the light remained on and the shoes made a diagonal trip across the room, gradually revealing a back view of trousers, suspender loops and a portion of tucked-in shirt. Another light switched on, and Ben's three-quarter-length perspective of West Ridgeman disappeared into an adjoining bath.

Sara nudged him in the ribs, and Ben rolled his head so he could look at her. "This is West's bedroom, isn't it?" she mouthed.

"Bingo," he mouthed back.

"What are we going to do?"

"We are going to hope he's a sound sleeper."

She grimaced, and Ben turned his head again to prevent her from seeing any hint of the amusement burgeoning inside him. It was understandable that Sara would have some difficulty seeing the humor in their situation, but he couldn't help himself. And to think he had nearly opted for a hotel room and an early night.

A few minutes later, the shower came on, followed by the clunk of the shower door closing, then quickly by a sharp pinch on his arm. He looked at Sara.

"He's in the shower," she whispered as she scooted out from under the bed. "Let's get out of here."

Ben grabbed for her, but she slipped out and away from his reach. With a sideways lunge, he just managed to get his hand around her ankle as she scrambled to her feet. She bent and peered under the bed. "What's wrong with you?" she hissed. "Come on."

"He's not in the shower yet." Ben tugged on her ankle. "He just turned it on."

Her brown eyes got wide and panic-filled. He released her, and she dropped to all fours beside the bed just as West Ridgeman—naked as far as Ben's eye could see—walked back into the bedroom.

and see. She bent and pe-red under the bed.
"Quite a web, wiliny ."] she liet . "Come and
look at the shower," the Ben urged at his
spider in that wicked cor. .

She turned as ever, with the pair t'al the He'd
given was to the dropped to all-ons trying. He had
run in all ingerselike] apped his , re is leg , and
spider . walked only he the bathroom.

Chapter Eight

"Sara?" West's voice was sharp with surprise. "What are you doing down there?"

With a gulp, she raised her head and wondered why he looked so scrawny without his clothes on. "Hi, there," she said thickly. "I was, uh, looking for...something." Uh-oh. What if he offered to help her look? "My, uh, glasses." Using the top of the mattress for balance, she pushed to her feet. "I was looking for my glasses. But as you can see, they're not under the bed." She winced as Ben pinched her little toe. "*Nothing*'s under the bed," she added hurriedly, and got another pinch for her trouble.

West took a step toward her. "You don't wear glasses, Sara."

"I don't?" This night was never going to end. "That must be the reason I didn't find them."

"Be honest, Sara. You sneaked into my room to try to make amends for tonight's disaster. You planned to surprise me into accepting your apology, didn't you?" His self-assurance was too slick, his tone too debonair for the scrawny body they represented.

With a blink, she brought up her gaze and made it focus on his face. "Believe me, if I had planned this, I wouldn't be here."

"You mean this is a spur-of-the-moment decision? An impetuous act based on an equally impetuous idea?"

"There's no reason to make it sound like a once-in-a-lifetime occurrence, West."

"Forgive me, but I am amazed—deeply flattered, of course, but still amazed to find you in my bedroom so unexpectedly. To be candid, Sara, I didn't believe you had an ounce of impulsiveness in you."

"It came over me very suddenly." How was she going to get out of this? "And, well, it just seemed like such a good idea at the time."

"It doesn't seem too bad, even now."

"I guess that depends on your perspective."

"Ah. There's no need to be nervous. You have my solemn promise that I will still respect you in the morning."

She could not believe he had said that. From the way Ben tweaked her toe, he obviously couldn't believe it, either. "Actually, respect isn't high on my priority list at the moment, West."

He looked startled, pleased, and particularly smug... not precisely in that order. "You're displaying hidden depths, Sara, and I have to tell you that my first reaction is pure delight. I was beginning to think you would never... warm up... so to speak."

Oh, boy. If Ben hadn't been under the bed, she might have warmed up to West a little more. But all she could think of was Ben under the bed, hearing every word, evaluating her ability to handle the situation, rating West's seduction techniques—and her responses—like an Olympic judge.

West advanced toward her with lust in his eyes and she prepared for a siege. "Did I mention how—and I mean this most sincerely—*sexy* you look in that tuxedo shirt? Not another woman at the party tonight could have worn that outfit and gotten away with it. And I guarantee that every man in the room was thinking the same thing I was."

His voice dropped dramatically as he reached her and, despite her better judgment, she had to ask, "What were you thinking, West?"

He chuckled. One of those short, soft laughs some men use to smooth over any possible offense that might be taken from his next remark. "I was wondering what color lingerie you were wearing underneath."

"Maybe I'm not wearing any." She moved her foot before Ben could tweak her toe again. He was going to get them both caught if he didn't stop that.

West all but drooled as he slipped an arm around her shoulders and put a hand on the button placket of her shirt. "And I'm the lucky man who is about to see for himself."

"Not so fast." She placed her hand over his. "You left your shower running."

"Let it run. I can afford to pay the water bill."

"But, West, there's plenty of time, and—" she traced her finger across his bare chest "—anticipation is half the pleasure, you know."

He caught her hand, raised it to his lips and kissed her palm. "You're quite the temptress tonight, Sara."

"I do seem to be on a roll." Ben Northcross was going to owe her a lot more than fifty cents for this rescue, she decided. "Take your shower, West. The mystery of what I'm wearing under this shirt can wait a little longer."

"I'm not sure I can wait another second." He jerked her against his naked body and bent his head to claim her lips in a sloppy kiss.

Sara allowed the embrace to continue just long enough for Ben to have time to wonder if he was going to be stuck under the bed during an entire love scene. Then she placed her palms against West's bare chest and pressed him back. "Go take your shower," she said in her best seductress whisper, making sure it was loud enough for Ben to overhear. "And when you come out, I'll be ready for you."

West ran his tongue across his lips then gathered her close and kissed her again. "Sara, Sara, Sara," he murmured a long moment later. "I may actually forgive you for wrecking the party and my house, after all. Why not come into the shower with me and earn a few extra brownie points by scrubbing my back?"

"That's so tempting, but I really had my heart set on surprising you."

"You already have. A thousand times over."

"I meant," she said hastily, "I want to be able to surprise you again."

"Totally unnecessary, love. You have persuaded me to be yours tonight...body and soul." He cupped her hips, then his hands sidled up her back...and stopped to investigate the long, ragged slit in her shirt. His smile ebbed slightly and his voice picked up the tone of a prosecuting attorney. "What happened to your shirt? How did it get torn like this?"

Sara could practically hear the ice breaking under her feet, but she tossed her hair, called up her best impression of sultry and aimed for his most vulnerable spot—his ego. "I tore it, West." Hoping she hadn't forgotten how, she batted her eyes at him. "I thought that would make it easier for you to rip it off."

There was a muffled thud under the bed, but West was too preoccupied to notice. "Oh, Sara, baby. So there was some planning involved, after all." He bent to kiss her again, but she put her fingers against his lips.

"Shower first," she whispered. "A hot, steamy body is such a turn-on."

"I'm not sure I can get much hotter."

"Of course you can," she murmured huskily, thinking that if this didn't work, she might have to resort to stuffing him in the shower by force. "Go take your shower. Please."

He backed away from her with a smile that stretched from ear to ear. "All right, but let the record show that I object to this delay."

She batted her eyes some more. "I love it when you talk legal to me."

"Defendant is hereby ordered to remain in this courtroom until tomorrow morning."

She nodded and waved.

"Discovery will begin after a short recess."

She blew him a kiss.

"I'll return to examine your briefs."

She wished she had an electric gavel to prod him into that shower. "Remember, hot and steamy. This is one case you won't want to lose."

He waggled his eyebrows, pursed his lips in a promised kiss and disappeared into the bathroom. Sara thought about following him...as soon as she smuggled Ben out of the room, that is. One night with West could cinch her future, pave the way for a marriage proposal. On the other hand, she hadn't planned this, hadn't thought it through. What if it was the wrong action to take? Worse, what if Ben waited for her in the van? Or in the kitchen? What if she couldn't keep her mind on West for worrying about where Ben was and what he was doing? As she heard the shower door open and close, followed by the changing rhythm of the spray, she made her decision. She leaned down and whispered, "Let's go!"

As Ben rolled out from under the bed, she raced to the door, cracked it open and glanced up and down the hall. Waving the all clear, she stepped out of the bedroom and waited for Ben to join her before she shut the door behind them.

"Was he wearing a necktie?" Ben asked.

"Not that I noticed, no."

"I suspected he was underdressed for the occasion."

"Well, he wasn't expecting company."

"What a diplomatic answer." Ben complimented her tact. "Any other woman would have made some tacky comment about his shortcomings."

"Could we talk about this later?"

"Sure, if you want to." He looked left, then right, then left again. "Which way is the exit?"

"Your guess is as good as mine." She chose a direction and took off in a hurried trot.

Ben hustled to keep up. "Well, at least you can truthfully say you've been in his bedroom now."

"Yes, well, so can you."

"This is just a hunch, but when he figures out you've fled his jurisdiction, *hot and steamy* is going to take on a whole new connotation."

"I know, I know, but it wasn't like I had the option of asking him to turn his back while you crawled out from under his bed."

"Let the record show that I thought you handled the situation magnificently. Ridgeman is going to spend an extremely restless night."

"So are we, if we don't get out of this hallway before he throws open that door and starts looking for me."

"Then we'd better hurry."

As if she needed to be reminded. Her life's plans were washing down the drain at this very moment. All because of that silly wedding gown. Temper rising, she reached the sweeping front stairway and ran down at a brisk trot.

Ben was on her heels when she made the second-floor landing, where greasy stains commemorated Cleo and Brody's roast-beast feast. His footsteps matched hers precisely as she reached the foyer, turned into the long living room, crossed the dining room and headed for the swinging door that led into the kitchen.

"You get the dress from Arthur's room and I'll stand watch."

"Forget the dress." Sara pushed past the kitchen door, barely noticing that the backward swing almost caught Ben square in the face. "I'll pay for it if I have to. I'll pay the fee you're supposed to get for delivering it. But under no circumstances am I going anywhere near it." She reached for the back-door knob.

"You'll set off the alarm," Ben warned.

She glanced at him over her shoulder. "Feel free to stay and offer my apologies."

Before she could turn the knob, the door opened from the outside and Arthur stepped in to greet them with a dispassionate gaze. "The boutique is closed," he said. "Unless, of course, you are here to return the clothes you borrowed."

"We were just on our way out," Sara said and moved to pass him.

"But since you're here," Ben said, then grabbed her hand and held tight, "we'd like to take the wedding gown with us."

Arthur nodded amicably. "You have my blessing."

"We'd prefer to have the dress."

Sara tugged, trying to pull free. "There isn't time for this," she muttered. "He'll be down here any minute."

"I assume Mr. West is aware you're in the house." Arthur started to close the door, but she caught it with her free hand.

"We're leaving now, Arthur, so if you wouldn't mind, tell him that something came up and I had to rush home. Or maybe you could tell him you didn't see me and thought I left a while ago. I know it's a lot to ask, but please, just this once, be a sport and cover for me." She jerked against Ben's restraint, tugging him off balance and out the door with her.

"I really don't want to leave that dress." He hurried to get his foot inside the doorway. "Listen, Artie, run up to your room and throw the wedding gown out the window. I'll catch it and everyone will be happy." He paused. "Well, not everyone, but three out of four ain't bad."

"I do not care to 'run up,' young man, nor do I throw articles of clothing out of windows. I will open the gate in five minutes, and if the two of you are not off the premises in ten, I will contact the security service. Good night." With that dismissal, Arthur closed the door.

Ben let go of Sara's hand and raised his fist to knock, but she grabbed it in time. "Will you stop that?" she said. "West will sue you for harassment."

"Me? You're the one who left him steamed up."

She hurried to the van, glancing back as he followed more slowly than she would have liked. "I hope you have the keys, because I really don't want to walk home."

"Especially not in that outfit." Ben dug into his pockets. "Patrolmen would be stopping to ask you what color underwear you have on."

Her temper warred with her urge to put a considerable distance between herself and this house. "Unless you feel the need for a midnight stroll across Kansas City, I'd suggest that you forget everything you overheard in West's bedroom tonight."

"Hmm, tall order, but I'll do my best." He pulled the keys from his pocket and held them up with a smile before he moved to unlock the driver's side door. "Hello, Cleo. Did you miss me?"

The Lab barked a sharp denial, and then barked some more.

Sara jerked the keys out of Ben's hand. "Make her hush, will you?"

"Speak, Cleo. Speak," he said, and the dog lapsed into immediate silence.

"See? Reverse psychology works best on her."

With a sigh, Sara looked at Ben's engaging grin. "Whatever you do, Ben, don't get in the van."

He climbed across the driver's seat and console without further delay. "What do you know?" he said. "It works on me, too."

Sara got in, inserted the key and turned the ignition. The engine didn't even sputter, and her heart plunged to a new low. "I don't believe this." She tried again with no better success. "I really don't believe this."

"Sounds like the battery is dead. Pop the hood and I'll take a look."

"What's the point? No matter what the problem is, I can't do anything about it now. And don't bother to suggest that I go back to the house and ask to use the phone."

"How about asking to use their battery cables?"

She looked at him and then laid her head against the back of the seat. "This has been the absolute worst day of my life."

"I'll bet you fifty cents that in an hour, you'll be laughing about it."

To her horror, she felt a teardrop slip from the corner of her eye and trickle down her cheek in utter and complete frustration.

With the utmost care, Ben caught the teardrop on his fingertip and held it up to the light beaming down from the upper corner of the house. "What do you know?" he said softly. "Reverse psychology works on you, too."

Wallowing in misery was not her style, so Sara took a deep breath and made a decision. Slipping the gear stick into neutral, she released the emergency brake and felt a spurt of accomplishment when the van rolled slowly forward.

"We're moving." Ben looked from her to the windshield and back to her. "But we appear to be moving toward the house, not away from it."

"I know that." She twisted the steering wheel as hard as she could, and the direction altered by a few degrees. "If I can just get this turned a little more..."

"I'm not sure what your plan is, but unless it involves cutting through the house, you might want to apply your brakes."

She struggled to wring another couple of inches from the steering wheel. "I'm trying to pick up speed, not slow down."

"And doing a fine job of it, too." His hands clamped onto the wheel, bracing her strength with his own, enhancing her effort with steady pressure.

The van turned, rolled faster and skimmed past the corner of the house with a quarter inch to spare. It bounced several times, then dropped five or six inches onto the driveway. Sara resolved not to think about which of the flower beds on this side of the house contained West's prize roses. Tomorrow would be soon enough to assess further damage. Right now, she just wanted to get herself and her van on the other side of that gate before she got closed in here for the duration of the night. She turned the wheel, but the van was slow to respond. It crossed the driveway and rolled onto the lawn. Water sloshed across the windshield as the sprinkler system's rotating heads made their midnight rounds. Realizing she had gone from compacting West's roses to crushing his meticulous lawn, Sara overadjusted and drove across the driveway and up onto another flower bed. There was a loud clunk and then a grating, groaning noise, which became a watery scrape, which in turn changed to a rhythmic thunk, thunk, thunk, thunk, thunk.

She twisted the wheel and appealed to Ben for assistance. "I'll give you my firstborn child if you can help me get this back on the pavement."

"That's a bit drastic. I'll settle for dinner, how's that?" He grabbed the wheel, wrested it to the right, held on through a series of bone-jarring and teeth-rattling bumps and grinds until the van corrected course and rolled steadily toward the gates at the end of the drive.

Releasing the wheel, Ben looked out the window, twisting in the seat to see behind them. He let out a long, low whistle.

"What is it? What did we hit?"

He resumed a forward-facing position and slumped slightly in the seat. "You don't want to know."

She glanced in the mirror. "I don't see anything unusual."

"Really? Well, that's good. Just try not to think about it."

"This is not a good time to tease me, Ben. Tell me what I did."

"You made it easier for Ridgeman to water his lawn, that's all. You probably did him a favor."

With a lift of her eyebrow, she demanded to know the whole sorry saga.

"The sound you heard was the sprinkler system being ripped from the ground like the pull string on a pack of chewing gum."

She quickly checked the mirror again, but saw only a haze of moisture reflecting off the house lights. "The sprinklers seem to be working."

"Overtime. The mist you see behind us is actually a geyser. Or rather, dozens of geysers spewing barrels of water over what may soon be Ridgeman Pond."

He had to be kidding. "That isn't funny, Ben. I feel bad enough about driving across West's lawn without your trying to make it seem worse than it is."

"I wasn't trying, Sara."

She checked his sincerity in a glance that sent her heart plunging to her toes. "You mean that noise *was* the sprinkler system? I did uproot it?"

"Afraid so."

Her moan was low and desperate as she checked the watery landscape in the side mirror. "West will never speak to me again as long as I live. I can't believe this. I really can't...." She frowned. "How much does a sprinkler system cost? On the average?"

"I don't know. Probably less than it's going to cost to repair your van."

"You're kidding. Less than the cost of replacing the car battery?"

"I didn't factor in a new battery."

"Oh. But the van's working."

"It's rolling. There's a difference."

She nodded unhappily. "Right. Well, once we're off the property, I'll call the automobile club and get a tow truck. At least we won't have to walk home."

Ben frowned and leaned forward. "I thought we had ten minutes to vacate the premises."

With a blink, Sara realized the gate was closing, and she automatically floored the gas pedal . . . which only increased her anxiety and did nothing to speed up the van. "Arthur said he'd give us ten minutes," she whispered in dismay. "Maybe if I honk the horn, he'll hear it and open the—" Her attempt to honk the horn met with futility, and she rattled the steering wheel in frustration. "Does anything around here still work?"

"The gate, apparently. Although I have a feeling that along with the sprinkler pipes, you probably unearthed the security-system wiring."

"Wouldn't that keep the gates from closing?"

"Not necessarily."

The iron gate shut with a resounding clank only seconds before the van rolled into it, bounced back, then rolled forward again and stopped, bumper to bars, just this side of the open road.

Ben rubbed his chin. "Do you realize there are people who don't experience this much excitement in their entire lifetime?"

"You may find this hard to believe, but until today, I was one of them."

Even before he turned to look at her, she knew he was fighting the impulse to laugh. Good humor leaked across the solemn line of his mouth and softened the crinkles around his eyes. As his lips gave in to the smile and his silence to a companionable chuckle, Sara recognized a similar response fighting its way past her misery. There was nothing remotely amusing about her situation, but in less than a heartbeat, she was laughing as if she hadn't just carelessly run over her future, as if she hadn't impulsively and inexplicably ruined her life. She didn't understand what was going on inside her head . . . or her heart. But suddenly, for no good reason she could fathom, her frustration dissolved into the buoyant, comforting sounds of Ben's laughter.

She laughed until her sides hurt, until the shambles of all her plans were covered in a dreamlike mist and seemed not so terribly important. When the laughter finally ebbed, she rubbed her eyes. "This isn't funny, you know."

"All I know is, this is the most fun I've ever had while wearing a tuxedo." His smile was sensual and sincere, and she couldn't help thinking that until now she had thought the two words were mutually exclusive.

"You're only wearing part of a tux," she said logically. "Only the shirt and bow tie."

"I think I'll design a line of formal wear based on the camouflage theme. 'For the well-dressed man, who wants to keep his legs covered.' Or, 'When it's important not to be seen.' Or how about, 'Only her legs should show.' What do you think?"

"I think you and your legs should slip through those iron bars and see if you can open the gate from the other side before Security shows up."

He glanced at the gate. "I'm in camouflage, Sara, not a rubber suit. But I couldn't squeeze through there if I was coated in three layers of vegetable oil. You're a lot smaller than I am. Couldn't you scrunch through the bars?''

''There are parts of my body that refuse to scrunch, no matter what kind of reward is offered. I may as well confess that I've never been able to do the splits or the Hokey Pokey.''

''I never would have guessed.''

With the pressing knowledge that the Security service was probably on its way, or the intimidating possibility that West himself would make an appearance, she jerked the handle and opened the door of the van. ''We'd better reassess our situation in a hurry, because from here the possibility of a happy ending looks like a washout.''

BEN RATTLED THE GATE—which held fast—then stepped back to study the wall of masonry that surrounded the house. Ridgeman had built a damned fortress.

Hands on her hips, Sara examined the pointed, javelinlike bars of this new obstacle to her plans. ''I'm not climbing over the gate, that's for sure.''

''I'm relieved to hear it—duck!'' They crouched beside the left front wheel as the spray from the only functioning sprinkler head oscillated past. As soon as the deluge of droplets moved on, Ben stood and reached for Sara's hand to help her up. ''There has to be a better way.''

He sensed a wry challenge in the look she gave him and was delighted that adversity only seemed to spark her fighting spirit.

"You know," she said, "this would be an ideal time to demonstrate your theory that real men are born with the right tools."

"I said they were born with all the tools they need. I didn't say they were born with the right tool for every occasion."

"Don't get testy. I just thought you might have a chisel in your pocket, that's all." She looked from him back to the gate. "Any chance you could pull those bars apart with your bare hands?"

"Not even if I had two Clydesdale horses to help me." He watched her, endlessly fascinated by her facial expressions, continuously amazed at her determination to do things her own way.

"Duck," she said. The sprinkler sent water over the top of the van in a pounding shower. When it moved on again, Sara fluffed her hair with her hands, shedding water drops like a dog after a soak. "I'm getting nearly as wet trying to keep from being sprinkled as I would be if I walked around the van and dared it to hit me."

"If I'd thought about it, I'd have brought along an umbrella."

She balanced on one foot and brushed a clump of mud from her ankle. "If I had an umbrella right now, I have no doubt that lightning would make a beeline for it."

"There isn't a cloud in the sky."

"Believe me, that is only because I am not holding anything remotely resembling a lightning rod."

Laughter rumbled in his throat. He couldn't recall the last time he had felt so alive. "In that case, you might want to avoid touching the gate, too."

"You're right." She reestablished her balance by setting both feet in the center of a trickling river that coursed down the drive and out the gate. "Maybe Cleo could squeeze through the bars and go for help."

Ben thought she might be developing a fever. "You must have her confused with Lassie."

"Look at her. She wants out of here as much as I do."

Cleo sat in the driver's seat of the van, watching the activity with a critical eye. "Yes," Ben said. "It's easy to see how desperate she is."

"Can you see how desperate I am? Does it show?"

"Not noticeably. Otherwise, you'd go back up to the house and ask for help."

"I would rather shinny up that cedar tree over there than face West again tonight."

"I don't see why. You didn't have any trouble seducing him a little while ago."

"I did not seduce him. I merely used the tools I was born with to escape from a rather delicate situation. And under no circumstances will I do another thing to imprint this disastrous night on his brain."

"When he has to swim down the driveway in the morning, I'm afraid he'll develop instant recall."

"Yes, but in the morning, I won't be here."

"I'll keep my fingers crossed for you. Duck." This time, as they huddled beside the van, Ben slipped a hand around her waist...ostensibly to steady her, but really because he couldn't keep from touching her. Her shiver translated itself into his body as desire, and he wished he could believe there was no other interpretation, that she, too, felt this bewildering and incontestable attraction. But she was wet and getting wetter, and her shiver indicated nothing other than a slight chill. He moved his arm to her shoulder and pulled her close. "We'll be out of here soon," he said. "I'm sure of it."

She looked at him, and his heart stopped. He had held enough women in his arms to know that his number had just come up. In Sara's russet brown eyes, he could see his future—a house with a porch swing, kids in the yard, Cleo at his feet, a redhead by his side. It was all there, within his grasp, waiting for him to claim....

"Ben? What are you doing?"

He took a long, deep breath. "Adjusting my perspective," he said. Then he lowered his head and kissed her.

Chapter Nine

Something happened the moment his lips closed over hers. The kiss, of course. She was well aware *that* was happening. But there was something else. Something unusual, strange, magical. Like the moment the dress had twinkled at her. She had been doing crazy things ever since, and now... Now Ben was kissing her. With purpose. With forethought. With devastating intent.

And damn it, she was kissing him back. With feeling.

Of their own accord, her hands slipped around his neck, and when he pushed to his feet, she moved with him. He pulled her against him and deepened the intensity and thoroughness of the kiss. A subsequent and serious yearning uncoiled inside her, like a spring stretched to the breaking point and then released. She felt giddy and dizzy, foolish and fanciful, drunk with a crazy, impulsive longing. This did not bode well for her plans, she thought.

Then she remembered she had no plans. Why not seize the moment? What the hell? Kissing Ben was the only pleasurable event of the entire evening, anyway.

His lips moved over hers, drawing desire to the surface. His arms gathered her against him, evoking a whole new awareness. His fingers grazed her skin beneath the raw edges of the rip in her shirt, and a heat wave of response radiated from that one touch. She imagined him ripping off the shirt, imagined his hands on her breasts, imagined him kindling the passion she had always suspected was smoldering inside her.

When the first drops of water showered over her, Sara thought she heard a sizzle, but a second later, the full force of the spray soaked her. And the heated kiss—along with the rest of her—cooled instantly.

Ben drew back, cupped his hands on either side of her nose and brushed the moisture from her face. The texture of his palms on her cheeks was both rough and soft and full of a gentle sensuality. The look in his deep green eyes left her weak and wanting...and wondering. She couldn't seem to catch her breath as he tucked strands of dripping hair behind her ears. "We forgot to duck," he said.

"It was your turn to warn me." Her words were so soft, he leaned closer to hear, which didn't help her voice get stronger as she repeated, "It was your turn to warn me."

He smiled and shook his head. "Let the record show that defendant was otherwise occupied and unaware of the impending shower. Therefore, defendant is not guilty of the premeditated crime of soaking the plaintiff."

"Overruled."

"Objection."

"You can't object to a ruling."

"You're the plaintiff. You can't make a ruling."

"That just shows how much you and I know about courtroom procedure."

"Speak for yourself. I went to law school."

Surprise restored her voice to full strength. "You're an attorney?"

"No, I just went to law school for a year, then I dropped out."

"Dropped out?" Her mouth dropped open. "Why?"

"It lost its *appeal*." He grinned at his joke.

Sara didn't. "I can't believe you had the chance to become a lawyer and you blew it."

His grin disappeared. "I didn't blow it, Sara. I got tired of using big words and I chose not to continue."

"You dropped out." She shook her head in disbelief. "What did you do after that? Apply to med school?"

"Actually, I did that before law school."

"You dropped out of med school, too?"

"I never went. My father wanted me to be a doctor, so I got accepted—just to prove that I could, I suppose. But I never really had any desire to study medicine."

"So what did you have a desire to study?"

"Architecture, but by the time I figured that out I was tired of school altogether, so I went to Australia and worked on a sheep station."

"Sheep?" She couldn't seem to conquer her astonishment. "You sheared sheep?"

"No. Mostly I cooked."

"What?"

"Oh, stews and casseroles, mainly. Once in a while, something more exotic."

"No, I meant, what, as in you're kidding."

"Oh. No. I'm not kidding. I'm pretty handy with food. You'll have to sample my cooking sometime."

Her interest whetted, she studied him with a new wariness. "What happened to that job? Did you lose your *taste* for it?"

"No, I developed a passion for soccer and conned a friend into letting me play on his team. I spent as much time on the sidelines as on the field, but I can truthfully say I've played professional soccer."

"And after that?"

His forehead creased with the effort of remembering. "Um, a few months crewing for one of those university-at-sea groups. Then a stint as a late-night DJ on a radio station in Honolulu. I worked as a ski instructor in Colorado for a short while. After that, I managed an art gallery in Santa Fe and then a restaurant in Detroit, and sometime in there I flew tourists over the Grand Canyon in a helicopter. I think that might have been before the art gallery."

As Sara stared at him, confused by this shift in her perspective, the sprinkler made another round, drenching them from head to toe and feeding the river of silt at their feet. She pushed the wet hair from her eyes and blinked, wishing she could lose all interest in the soggy, sexy man standing before her. But even dripping wet, in the midst of her dire predicament, curiosity got the best of her. "All right," she said. "Give it to me straight. How many careers have you abandoned because you got bored?"

He shrugged. "I haven't kept count. Usually I lose interest in an activity as soon as I've proven to myself

I can do it. When there's no further challenge, the risk is gone and so am I.''

"What kind of time frame are we talking from spark of interest to the last goodbye?"

He leaned against the van, crossed his arms and considered. "I've been doing stunt work for movies and television for the past four years. That's probably the closest I've come to steady employment."

"Don't you think about security? Retirement? Planning for the future?"

"Security, never. Retirement, only when I'm physically exhausted. Planning for the future? That's a very recent consideration."

His eyes locked on hers for a heartbeat, and her breath deserted her like a fleeting thought. The magic wove through her like a satin ribbon, and she was tempted—oh, so tempted—to let this mystical attraction take her where it would. But Ben was the wrong kind of man, the kind she always fell for—a traveling salesman of dreams. A man with no need for stability or roots. A man who would forever be on his way to the next rainbow.

Unfortunately for her, he was also a man whose smile took away her breath, whose kisses stole her reason. And right now, she needed both her ability to breathe and to think clearly.

She was not, under any circumstances, going to get involved with a man who had no better ambition than to follow his attention span wherever it roamed. An uncertain future was exactly what she had known all her life, the very thing she was determined never to know again. She had struggled too hard and planned too well to let a physical attraction overshadow her goals. And no amount of desperate kisses could change her mind.

She turned abruptly, moving away from the promise of soul-stirring passion and toward the gate. "I wonder if there's a release somewhere that allows this to be opened manually."

"Good thinking, Sara." He moved past her to investigate. "And here it is. A manual release—and it's secured with a padlock. Ridgeman must be a fanatic."

"He's very careful, that's all." Defending West wasn't anything she felt particularly compelled to do, it just seemed better than not defending him and tacitly agreeing he was a bit of a fanatic. "I like caution in a man."

Ben's gaze caught hers in the damp and dusky dark, and his brief silence teemed with a challenge she half hoped he'd issue. But he stooped to examine the padlock instead.

Aware of a sharp twinge of disappointment, she turned her head and met Cleo's softly accusing eyes through the van window. "Ah, are you tired of being cooped up in there?"

The moment Sara opened the door, the Lab bounded out and trotted to the gate, stopping only long enough to shake off some water after the sprinkler passed over.

"She's feeling better."

Ben didn't answer. He glanced at Cleo as she took a position beside him. "I'm working on it," he said to the dog, as if she had demanded to know why he hadn't opened the gate for her.

There was affection there, between the dog and the man. Sara could see it, no matter how much Ben claimed there was no love lost. She wondered if it had evolved from their separate relationships with the other woman . . . or if it had grown from their mutual respect for the other's independence. Choosing the latter—because she did not want to think about Ben and that woman—she started to close the driver's side door before the next pass of the sprinkler. But a streetlight, refracted through the spray of water, caught her attention and she paused.

The wall really wasn't that high. A pole vault athlete could probably clear it easily. Of course, she didn't have a pole and her body wasn't Olympic material . . . but she had the next best thing to a stepping stool. All she had to do was push the van away from the gate and line it up beside the wall.

Her spirits improved as she assessed the possibility. "I have an idea," she said. "Help me move the van."

Ben barely glanced at her. "What did you say?"

"I'm going to push the van back and roll it close to the fence. That way we can climb up and jump down on the other side."

Man and Labrador turned in unison to stare at her.

"Oh, don't be so negative," she said. "This will work. Trust me. All you have to do is push."

"I don't think so."

"All right, Doubting Thomas, you get in the van and steer while I push." She moved to the front fender, which was flush against the gate, and gave it a hefty shove.

"Unless you want to be paper thin in about two seconds, I'd suggest you stop trying to defy the laws of gravity."

"What do you know about laws?" she said smugly as the van moved a bit. "You dropped out of school."

He grabbed her shoulders and pulled her away from the front of the van. "Not before I learned that if you roll something uphill, it's going to roll downhill again."

Sure enough, the van retraced the few inches gained and clanked into the gate. Ignoring the warm, safe feeling his protectiveness evoked in favor of a fierce determination to prove her point, she concentrated on how to accomplish her immediate goal as quickly as possible. "If you'd been in the van, *as I asked,* it would have turned easily, and we'd be halfway home by now."

He frowned at her. "There's another way—"

"*Don't* say it. If there was another way out of this place, I'd have found it by now. Just humor me. Get in the van and steer."

There was a moment when she thought he was going to argue, but she lifted her chin to suggest the futility of such an action, and he simply shrugged. "I'll help you on one condition. I'll turn the steering wheel and we'll both push. Agreed?"

"That isn't necessary," she began, but she knew it probably was. "All right. If you insist."

He nodded. "I do. And, just as another matter of natural law, it will be more effective to push on the opposite fender."

She immediately saw the logic in that, although she maintained an indifferent expression. As he climbed inside and set the wheels, Sara dashed around the van, past the crumpled A Vice side panel, to reach the right front fender. Realistically, she knew her strength alone probably wasn't up to the task. But as an example of her determination, one push couldn't hurt.

It didn't hurt, actually, but only because she landed, splat, in a puddle that somewhat cushioned the blow to her backside.

"Couldn't you have waited for me to come around here to help?" Ben asked a minute later as he extended a hand to her. "You didn't even give me time to get my foot off the brake."

Her dignity was bruised but not defeated, and Sara accepted his assistance in cool silence. Resisting the idea of shaking off the wetness with an all-over shudder, like Cleo would have done, Sara reached behind her and tugged on the tails of her shirt. The mud-plastered fabric peeled away from her skin with an embarrassing smacking noise and left a layer of gooey moisture across her back as thick as wallpaper paste. "If there's a law of nature about how many catastrophes can occur to one person in an alloted amount of time, I'd like to hear it."

Ben, wisely, did not smile. "That must have been covered in one of the classes I missed."

"Yes," Sara said. "For me, too."

TWO MINUTES later, the van rolled into position, scraping paint a good fifteen feet or so along the brick wall, yanking the last sprinkler head out of the ground, and uprooting a sapling before it stopped and sank to the hubcaps in the newly-forming Ridgeman Swamp.

"I can't believe this," she said, examining the new ruts. "I have never done anything so destructive in my life."

"It was an accident," he said.

"I don't have accidents," she countered just as quickly. "At least, I never did before I put on that dumb dress." Hands on hips, she surveyed the damage she'd left in her wake. Then she sighed with regret. "West will never speak to me again."

Following her gaze across the lawn, Ben figured her concern was unfounded. West Ridgeman, Attorney at Law, would be talking to her quite soon and probably none too quietly, either. But Sara, being Sara, remained focused on her plan—getting over the fence and out of Ridgeman's jurisdiction before she made any final decisions about what apologies to make and what reparations to offer.

He watched her as she climbed onto the roof of the van and prepared to boost herself up onto the wall. "Come on up," she called down. "You can't hurt this van, believe me."

He believed her, all right, but from this angle, he had an outstanding view of her legs, could even see the line of silk at the base of her hips. "Sara," he said. "There's something I should tell you."

"Now?"

"Yes." Lifting his gaze, he met her eyes with absolute sincerity. "I want you to know that not once during this entire evening did I wonder what color lingerie you were wearing."

"They're mud brown, at the moment. But thanks for telling me. It's good to know that you, at least, are a gentleman."

He resolved, then and there, never to confess the truth—that he'd had no reason to wonder. He'd known the color from the moment he unbuttoned the wedding dress in the van. "Be careful," he advised, as she swung one leg up and levered herself onto the wall. "Lower yourself first, then drop on the other side. Don't jump."

"You're the stuntman. Shouldn't you show me how it's done?"

"I have to get Cleo out. Besides, I know you're determined to do this your way, no matter what."

A look of concern replaced her smile. "I didn't think about Cleo. How are you going to get her on top of the van?"

"I'm not."

Sara sat on the wall, scooted around and started to ease over the other side. "You can't leave her here."

"I don't intend to." Ben strolled over to the gate, wincing as he heard the snap of branches, a muffled ouch and then a thud.

"Oooch." Sara limped into view. "I should have looked before I leaped. There are shrubs along the outside of the fence. You'll want to compensate for that when you drop over."

Extracting a compact knife from his pants' pocket, Ben stooped and picked the lock on the manual release. A moment later, he and Cleo walked through the open gate to join Sara on the other side.

"I TRIED TO TELL YOU, but you said, and I quote, 'If there was another way out of this place, I'd have found it,' end quote. I rest my case." Ben kept his pace steady with Sara's as they approached a cross street.

"Cleo, don't play in traffic." The dog didn't acknowledge his command, but she stopped at the curb nonetheless. He checked for traffic in both directions, but the streets weren't heavily traveled at this time of night. "Coast is clear," he said.

"Not for you, it isn't." Sara's shoulders were back, her chin was high, and her bedraggled appearance had an almost haughty dignity. "And don't try any of that reverse psychology stuff on me. At this point, getting hit by a car would be anticlimactic."

"I don't understand why you're still angry. Four blocks ago, I understood. Even two blocks back, I could feel some sympathy. But we have now walked eight full blocks from the Ridgeman estate, and frankly, it's time to change the subject."

"Easy for you to say. I'm hobbling and you're not."

"I have shoes and you don't. That isn't my fault, either. Look, Sara, I love the way you attack problems. I love the fact that you would rather do something the wrong way than stand back and do nothing at all. Or wait for someone else to do it for you. I respect your independent spirit, and I believe it would be both presumptuous and wrong to try to stop you from solving your own problems in your own way. Now, can we talk about something else?"

"Only if you promise that the next time I'm about to jump over a fence, you'll stop me. Agreed?"

She intrigued him with the hint of a smile, teased him with a toss of her wet hair, stole his heart with the daredevil glint in her eyes. "Agreed."

"You have to promise."

Ben knew he shouldn't, but the words pushed right past his better judgment. "I promise."

"Good. Now I don't have to think about that any-more."

"I'm relieved to hear it."

"I just have to figure out where the nearest phone booth might be." She didn't even stop at the curb, just vaguely glanced in both directions and kept walking. "Oh, geez, I should have remembered to get my purse out of the van. I don't have any money. Do you know if I can call collect from a pay phone or do I still have to put in a quarter first?"

"I'll loan you a quarter."

She nodded and stopped limping.

THANK YOU for coming to get us," Ben said.

"No problem. I can't sleep, anyway." Gypsy made another adjustment to her seat, giving her big belly more room behind the steering wheel and further cramping Sara, who was hunched down in the cargo section of the two-seater hatchback next to Cleo, who took up more than her alloted space.

"It doesn't make any difference whether I lay on my back or my side," Gypsy continued. "The baby kicks and keeps me awake. And to be perfectly honest, I'll take any excuse to get behind the wheel. I've always had a love affair with this car and Kevin won't let me drive it until after the baby's born. This way he'll never even know I was out of the house. You okay back there, Sara?"

"Fine." She wasn't, but there was no point in say-ing so and then having to describe every humiliating detail of the evening to Gypsy's satisfaction. "Just fine."

"What happened to your dress?" Gypsy angled herself in the seat and pressed the clutch, then angled the other way to press the gas pedal. The car lurched forward, shuddered and died. She twisted in the seat and started the procedure over again. "You know, the wedding gown? The one that twinkled at you."

Sara winced. "I took it off. You know, Gypsy, you and Ben have something in common. He was a cook at one time."

"Really?" Her blond head bobbed in Ben's direction as the transmission caught in first and the car edged forward. "You don't look like a cook."

"You don't look like a chauffeur."

Gypsy giggled. "I look like a Sumo wrestler, but that doesn't mean I am one." She shifted into second and then quickly into third. "I'm actually not much of a cook, either."

"You're just being modest," Sara offered from the back in the interest of keeping the subject rolling. "She's made some very unusual dishes."

Gypsy sighed. "Yes. Tonight, for instance, I fixed torched chicken."

"I've never heard of that. Was it good?"

"Well, the firemen loved it."

"Firemen?"

"I was over at Sara's house, you see, trying to unbutton the wedding gown so she could get out of it, and when I went to wash the Popsicle juice off my fingers, I saw the flames and knew dinner would be delayed."

"Did you set the house on fire?" Ben asked with concern.

"No. After the first fire, Kevin installed a smoke alarm with a direct wire to the fire station. My torched chicken was thoroughly foamed before I could waddle across the yard."

"I guess there was no way to salvage dinner at that point."

No way to salvage her life, at this point, either, Sara thought. Not after West woke up to a view of his new landscape. How could she have done such a thing? Would West ever believe that she'd meant no harm, that she had been the victim of a twinkling dress? Not much chance he'd buy that theory. No, she'd have to figure out some other, more believable way to apologize. If, of course, he ever spoke to her again....

"The firemen said they'd take it to the station and dispose of it, but I just had them bury it in the backyard."

"Beside numerous other entrées," Sara said, wanting to keep the conversation far away from the twinkling wedding dress and her dismal thoughts about West Ridgeman. "She burns dinner every Friday. You'd think Kevin would catch on, but so far..."

"He sounds like a prince of a guy." Ben looked over his shoulder. "So, Sara," he said. "How many people tried to get you out of that wedding dress before I came along?"

"MAKE YOURSELF at home." Sara switched on a lamp and whisked a candy wrapper and soda can off the coffee table. "Looks like Jason has been here and left again. Feel free to wander through the kitchen. You're welcome to anything you find. There's milk in the fridge, or at least there was earlier in the day. You can make yourself a sandwich or a cup of coffee, if you want.'' She was chattering, something she rarely did, and if it wasn't because she and Ben were alone in her house, she couldn't imagine what else it might be. Unless it was a reaction to the total mess she'd made of her life plans in one swoop. Make that one fatal *twinkle*. ''You and Cleo make yourself at home while I go into my office and write out your check.''

He nodded and walked to the couch. ''Thanks, we'll just sit, if you don't mind.''

''Sure. Sit. It will only take a minute to get the check ready.'' She started down the hall. ''Where are you staying tonight? Is it far from here?''

''I don't know.'' He raised his voice so it would reach her in her office. ''Where's the nearest motel?''

''Um, fifteen, twenty minutes back toward downtown. That's a rather pricey area, though. I doubt you'll find a room there for less than a hundred and fifty.''

''What a coincidence,'' he said. ''I already have the fifty. At least I will as soon as you pay back the quarter you borrowed for the phone.''

''It's one hundred and fifty dollars,'' she corrected. ''Not a hundred and fifty cents.''

There was a pause and then a patient, ''I knew that. I was making a little joke.''

''Oh. I guess I'm a little tired for subtlety.'' Pulling the At Your Service checkbook from the drawer of her desk, Sara wondered where he could cash a check at this time of night. But she didn't have a hundred dollars in cash to give him. She wasn't entirely certain she had a quarter. And his credit card had expired. And it was very late. And she needed to figure out how she could explain her actions to West. And she had to come up with a reasonable excuse for leaving him naked and steamed in his bedroom . . . a totally insane waste of an opportunity she realized, now that it was too late. There was either a full moon out or the twinkling wedding dress had stripped her of every vestige of good sense. She was exhausted just thinking about it. Ben had to be exhausted, too. But no. She could not and would not, invite him to spend what was left of the night here . . . with her.

"We'll look in the phone book," she said half to herself, verbalizing a plan more for her benefit than his. "There's bound to be an inexpensive motel somewhere in the area." She wrote out the check, tore it carefully from the stub and carried it with her to the front room. "Here's your . . ."

Her visitors had taken her at her word and made themselves at home. Cleo was snoozing, all curled up and obviously comfortable in the armchair. Ben was stretched out on the sofa, one arm covering his eyes, one across his waist. She could see by the rise and fall of his chest that his breathing was slow and steady. If he wasn't already, he was almost asleep. And despite knowing it was a bad—a very bad—idea to let him stay the night, she didn't have the heart to wake him up and tell him he had to leave.

With a sigh, she switched off the lights, turned on her heel and carried the hundred-dollar check with her down the hall and into her bedroom.

ON THE COUCH, Ben lay very still, concentrating on keeping his breathing slow and even. He was a little surprised at himself for resorting to subterfuge in order to stay the night at Sara's house. He could have refused to leave without the wedding dress. That was a perfectly legitimate excuse. Or he could have played up this idea she had that he was down on his luck and didn't know where his next meal was coming from.

But he was reluctant to add anxiety to her exhaustion. Tomorrow would be soon enough to decide how he would elicit an invitation to stay on for a while. One way or another, though, he was staying. And by the end of the week, if not sooner, she wouldn't be able to recall the name West Ridgeman.

Ben smiled with anticipation. It would be his name on her lips, his life she wanted to share, his arms she wanted to be in. All her plans were about to change. Just as all his plans had changed the moment she flew through the doorway and into his arms.

He'd reconciled to the probability that he would never find the woman who could coax a lifetime commitment from his heart. But in a split second, the odds had changed in his favor. One minute he'd been complacently headed for the next turn in the road, preparing to seek out a new adventure, pursue another temporary thrill...and the next minute, his arms were full of Sara and his heart was in a spin.

A spin he believed would never stop.

He had always suspected that love didn't operate on a time schedule and that it could happen as easily in an instant as in a year. What he hadn't counted on was that when it happened to him, there wouldn't be a reciprocal reaction from the woman.

On the other hand, he loved a challenge. And Sara was most definitely the challenge of his lifetime.

Chapter Ten

"Morning."

Ben looked up from his orange juice to encounter the curious stare of the young man who had just shuffled into the kitchen. "Morning," he answered as he noted the wrinkled clothing and the belligerent pair of brown eyes below a mop of tousled auburn hair and concluded that Sara's brother was just returning home after what must have been a boisterous night. "I'm Ben Northcross."

"Jason Gunnerson," came the mumbled reply. "That your Harley parked out by the curb?"

"Yes. She's a 1955 Panhead. Fifty-four thousand original miles."

Jason whistled. "Where did you find it?"

"In a barn in Tennessee. I made the farmer an offer on the spot. It took two days and several counteroffers, but I finally persuaded him to sell. Two weeks later, I had the engine up and running, and I'm going to do the bodywork once I get home. A year from now, she'll look and sound like she just rolled off the factory floor."

"Man. You're so lucky. I'd love to do something like that."

As Jason looked in one cabinet after another, Ben finished the orange juice, thinking that his whole life could be summed up in those two words. *You're lucky.* With all the risks he'd taken—some of them incredibly foolish—he was lucky to be alive. And healthy. And successful. With a little change in luck, it could easily have been he standing in this kitchen wishing for a motorcycle but not really believing he could ever hope to own one.

Jason closed a cabinet door, yawned, stretched and looked at the dog. "That your Labrador?"

"Her name is Cleo. She's waiting for breakfast."

"Yeah, well, good luck. No one cooks around this joint." Jason opened the refrigerator and poked his head inside. "I haven't had a decent meal since I got here."

"You should learn to cook."

"Yeah, right. Like Sara gives me free time to mess around in the kitchen."

"Works you pretty hard, does she?"

"Yeah." Jason tipped the milk carton to his mouth and drank in long, loud gulps. He swiped his hand across his lips, then set the carton, spout still open, back inside the refrigerator. "What's that smell?"

"A breakfast casserole. Makes you hungry, doesn't it?"

"Yeah. Where'd it come from? Did Sara get up and cook for you?"

"No, I made it. I haven't seen Sara this morning."

"Then take my advice and get out of here before she barrels in with a list of things a mile long for you to do." He shut the refrigerator door and looked Ben over. "Did she hire you last night?"

"Uh-huh."

"That figures. One screwup that wasn't even my fault, and she gives away my job." He ran his fingers through hair the same shade as Sara's and shook his head in frustration. "Sisters are nothing but a pain in the butt."

"Occasionally they do something redeeming."

"You got one?"

"Yes. A younger sister."

"You like her?"

"Most of the time."

Jason nodded slowly. "Yeah, I like Sara, too, most of the time. But lately she's always on my back, and she doesn't even give me a chance, you know. I try, but nothing's ever good enough to suit her. I should try harder or be smarter or have more ambition. That's her favorite gripe. You have no ambition. That's what she says."

"I'm sure she wants the best for you."

"Yeah, but I don't know how she thinks she can know what that is. Half the time, *I* don't even know."

"It's a matter of perspective, I imagine." Ben stood and walked across the kitchen. Covering his hand with a mitt, he opened the oven door and pulled out a pan, which he carried to the table. "Sit down," he said to Jason, "and I'll tell you how to cook this for yourself the next time you want a decent meal."

As Ben went over the recipe, Jason pulled out a chair, tipped it back, straddled it and then plopped down. He was scooping a huge serving onto his plate before the front chair legs regained the floor. By the time Ben returned to his place at the table with his coffee cup, the casserole was half gone.

"This is great," Jason mumbled around a mouthful of scrambled egg. "You're a pretty good cook."

"Thanks." Ben helped himself to a serving and watched Sara's brother plow into a second helping. Jason might have no idea where he was going, but he was in a hurry to get there, just the same. "Cooking isn't hard."

"You should tell that to Sara."

"I'm telling you."

Scraping the last bit of casserole from his plate, Jason finished eating, got up and took the carton of milk from the refrigerator again. This time he poured the milk into a glass before downing it in a long swallow. "How long you planning to stay around?" he asked.

"That depends."

Jason nodded as if he understood completely. "I hope she lets you stay long enough to cook dinner. Don't pay too much attention to anything she says, and you'll get along fine."

Ben observed him thoughtfully. "What do you think about West Ridgeman as a brother-in-law?"

"Couldn't say. Never met him, but Sara talks about him a lot. How successful he is and stuff like that. Personally, I think the main reason she's so impressed is because he's nothing like our old man."

"Your father?"

"Yeah, dear old Dad."

"He wasn't successful?"

Jason laughed, although without much humor. "Hardly. We must have moved a thousand times just because he'd hear about some new get-rich-quick idea or gimmick and had to get in on the ground floor. The last time Sara got a letter from him, he was somewhere in Mexico, selling vitamins and still waiting for his ship to come in."

Ben placed that piece of information into the puzzle that was Sara. "You and your sister didn't have a particularly stable childhood, I take it."

"Oh, I don't know. It didn't seem all that bad to me. But then, Sara was always there to make sure I had what I needed. She was kind of like my parent, I guess. A mother and father rolled into one person." He straightened from a boneless slouch. "I'm getting out of here before she catches me and sends me off on some stupid job. Man, I'd like to send her on a long vacation."

"Be careful what you wish for," Ben advised. "She may leave you in charge of At Your Service."

"Don't I wish. But that ain't never gonna happen." In its way, his youthful grin was as engaging as Sara's smile. "Thanks for the breakfast." He headed for the door. "Don't tell her you saw me. She'll just get mad at you for not havin' enough ambition to stop me from leaving." He leaned down to scratch Cleo's ear on his way past. "Bye, Cleo. You're a great dog." He looked at Ben. "What did you say your name was?"

"Ben Northcross."

"Nice to have met you." Jason walked away, moving quickly toward wherever he was going. A few minutes later, the front door opened and shut. A few minutes after that, a car engine coughed, sputtered, then caught with a rattling growl. The sound of a pulsating engine and a booming radio faded into the early noise of a Saturday morning in the suburbs.

Sipping his coffee, Ben thought about Sara as a young girl, assuming the responsibility for being both father and mother to her younger brother. He wondered where her mother had been, and how her father's success fantasies—if that's what they had been—had shaped her ambition. It was easy to see the source of her determination. She would never be content to sit back and daydream about the day her ship would come in. She'd swim out to meet it and drag it in by the anchor, if she had to.

And he intended to stay close to her, making sure she didn't drag in the wrong ship. Or the right ship for the wrong reasons.

"Nine-thirty!"

Like a warning bell at a railroad crossing, Sara's shout of dismay signaled the start of another round of surprises. Cleo lifted her head and looked at him, as if to ask, "What now?"

Ben shrugged in answer. "Whatever it is, I'm going along for the ride. And you may as well forget coming along as a chaperone. With or without reverse psychology, you're not invited."

With a dispassionate sigh, Cleo laid her head on her paws and closed her eyes.

SARA ENTERED the kitchen like a whirlwind, grabbed a coffee cup, and in a matter of sixty seconds or less had poured coffee, swallowed it, rinsed out the cup and set it in the dishwasher. In a slim-skirted dress of moss-green silk, she looked like a long-stemmed rose—delicate, dainty and adorned with some thorns.

"Have you seen Jason?" The words were rushed, the voice tense, the attitude clearly on the testy side.

"Your brother?"

"He would be the person who used that plate—" she pointed at the table setting "—to eat that—" her finger indicated the casserole dish "—before and after he drank milk straight from the carton." She picked up the empty milk carton and tossed it in the trash.

"As a matter of fact, there was someone like that here just a minute ago. But he used a glass."

"No, he didn't."

"The second time, he did."

Sara rolled her eyes. "That could ruin his reputation. Did he say where he was going?"

"No, but then I didn't ask."

"You should have. I'm running late, you know."

"I thought I recognized the symptoms."

She took another cup from the cupboard, poured a little coffee into it, drank it in a single swallow, rinsed the cup and set it in the dishwasher. "Do you realize that until yesterday, At Your Service had a perfect punctual attendance record? Now, suddenly, I'm late for everything."

"What are you late for this morning?"

"I've got to drive downtown, get Alicia Randolph's wedding gown and have it at the church by ten-thirty. I promised I'd have it there at ten, but I doubt I can manage that even if I drive like a maniac."

"And you wouldn't want to ruin your driving record."

She opened the refrigerator, took out the orange juice, poured it in a glass and drank it. "I don't suppose you'd be interested in being my assistant today, would you?" she said as she rinsed the glass and put it in the dishwasher. "Since my brother didn't see fit to stick around, I'm going to need some help."

"Do I get to unbutton that dress for you?"

"Absolutely not." She frowned at him, as if that would convince him of her seriousness. "This is business. Strictly business."

"In that case, I accept your offer of employment on one condition—I'll work for food."

"You mean, groceries?"

"I mean dinner. Tonight. I'll even cook."

She looked surprised. "Really? But you already cooked breakfast."

"I was hungry. Tonight will be for you."

An odd expression came into her eyes—not quite a smile, but a pleased look, as if no one had ever offered to cook for her before. "Okay." The acceptance was softly appreciative, quietly shy. Then she seemed to realize that time was sweeping past. Grabbing another cup from the cupboard, she poured a swallow of coffee, downed it, then rinsed the cup and set it in the sink instead of the dishwasher.

A change in routine, Ben thought. Interesting.

"Let's go." She headed for the front door, her shapely legs even more evocative through the long back slit in the slim, calf-length dress.

Ben didn't get up. Sara obviously hadn't realized the obstacles she was up against this morning.

"Oh, no!"

Obstacle one. Ben stood and strolled over to set his coffee cup in the sink—without rinsing it.

"The van is still at West's." She was back in the kitchen, anxiety pouring from every pore. "I'll have to call a taxi. Darn Jason. Why couldn't he have—"

The phone rang, and Ben had never seen anyone in such a hurry to answer.

"Sara Gunnerson, At Your Service."

Ben leaned against the kitchen counter and admired Sara's legs—along with the rest of her—while she was otherwise occupied.

"Gypsy," Sara said in a voice of measurable relief. "You don't know how glad I am to hear from you. I need to borrow your car." There was a pause. "It isn't? You're not? Where are you?" She caught Ben's eye and mouthed the word hospital. Then she said it aloud, as if the meaning just dawned on her. "Hospital? But the baby isn't due for another week! Okay, yes, I know babies can come early, but... Well, of course, I'm excited and I'll be there as soon as... Oh, that long? I guess I'll call you from the church, then... The Randolph wedding, that's right... Yes... And you're sure Kevin is on his way from the office? I know he wouldn't miss this... Gypsy? Please don't name the baby Tadpole." She replaced the phone receiver in the wall cradle and turned to Ben with a dazed and wondering expression. "Gypsy is having a baby."

"That's good news."

"Yes, but... a baby. A real baby. That's such an enormous responsibility, and Gypsy is so... inexperienced."

Ben smiled. "I read somewhere that with the birth of the baby, the mother is born."

Sara nodded, then sighed. "I suppose if the baby is lucky, that's true." She moved toward him, reaching for the cabinet door, but then her eyes met his and awareness flooded the kitchen like morning light. Startled, she withdrew her hand and smoothed her palm down the front of her dress. "I can't imagine that I would be very good at mothering."

"I can't imagine that you wouldn't." They would have a baby, he decided. An auburn-haired bundle of surprises, like her mother. The future was beginning to form in his mind with the luster of reality, and he knew he was a lucky, lucky man. "When the time comes, of course."

"Time." She glanced at the clock. "I've got to hurry. I wonder how long it will take to get a taxi over here. Maybe I could page Jason . . ."

Ben took her hand and led her to the front door while she continued to sort aloud through her options, trying to form a plan. Her frustration had barely warmed the morning air before he had her by the elbow and was escorting her to the only vehicle in sight. "We'll take my motorcycle," he said. "She's not pretty, but she's fast."

"I can't ride in that."

"The sidecar? Sure you can. Cleo does it all the time. You'll have to wear a helmet, but at least I'll get you to the church on time."

"Look at this dress. Even with the kick pleat in the back, there is no way I can get this skirt high enough on my thighs to let me step into that thing, much less ride comfortably."

"Who said anything about comfort?" Ben asked. "This is strictly transportation. No frills, no touches of luxury. Just plenty of thrills and the pulse of a powerful engine."

"And the wind in my hair. I can't arrive at the wedding on a motorcycle."

"In a sidecar. There is a difference."

She arched her brows in denial.

"Suit yourself, but it's here and available."

She looked at the cycle with distaste. "I have a feeling I'm going to really regret this."

"What would life be without a few regrets? Hike up your skirt and climb in. I promise, you're going to love this."

SHE DIDN'T LOVE wind whistling past the helmet he insisted she wear. And she didn't love the rattle and clatter of the sidecar bumping over the road. And she did not love the roar of the engine in her ears. But, other than that, the motorcycle ride was exciting.

There had to be an easier way to transport a wedding gown from the dry cleaner to the church, though. And there was undoubtedly a better method of dressing for this mode of travel. But she did have a great view. From this perspective, the traffic around them seemed like lumbering crates, all closed up and limiting. And when she turned her head ever so slightly, she could study Ben in profile, all the way from his classically chiseled chin past the T-shirt and jeans he was wearing to the tip of his scuffed black boot.

A funny tickle of a feeling stirred in her stomach. A feeling she quickly labeled physical appeal and shelved with other such fleeting attractions. But her mind kept returning to the image of a hospital, a woman, her husband, waiting for their baby to be born. She tried to insist to herself that it was Gypsy and Kevin she imagined, but the picture she saw was of herself, holding a dark-haired, green-eyed baby while Ben stood by, holding both of their hands.

Which was about the most ridiculous thing she could be thinking at the moment. Her life had taken a sudden sharp turn, and it was up to her to see that it got back on track without further delay. Alicia Randolph's wedding would go off without a hitch, because Sara had planned it to perfection. And she would be there—slightly behind schedule—to make sure everything went as planned. After that, she'd visit Gypsy, Kevin and the new little Collins. She paused in her planning to send up a little prayer on the baby's behalf. *Please don't let her name this baby. Let Kevin give all the information for the birth certificate.*

After that, she'd do the bank deposit and drop it in the night depository. And after that, she would sit down and think about how to salvage the damage she'd done to her relationship with West. The moment was fast approaching when she would have to face him and the consequences of her impulsive actions, if only because she had to pick up that silly wedding dress so Ben could finally be on his way.

He didn't seem to be in a hurry to leave. Probably glad to have a little extra cash in his pockets. But the wedding gown would have to be delivered to its intended bride sooner or later, even if the thought of Ben's leaving bothered her more than she cared to admit. He was just a guy. A nice, attractive, easy-to-be-with, resourceful guy, who had arrived on her doorstep at the wrong moment. Any kind of love-at-first-sight thing was pure fantasy. It didn't happen. And even if it did, she wouldn't consider a relationship with Ben, charming as he was. The last thing she needed in her life was a down-on-his-luck, unemployed adventurer.

The motorcycle changed lanes and Sara got plastered with a face full of Alicia Randolph's wedding gown. She fought with the wind, pressing one section of the billowing, plastic-covered wedding dress into her lap, only to have to struggle with another section that popped up. When she finally got everything tucked away out of the wind, she realized they'd missed their exit.

She tugged on Ben's sleeve, pointed, and he nodded. A moment later, the motorcycle picked up speed, dodged across the right lane of traffic and rocketed down the next exit ramp. At least, Sara hoped it was the ramp. She couldn't see for having to swat bridal gown out of her face.

"WELL, WELL, WELL. It's a small world, isn't it?" The police officer had pulled them over two blocks from the church. The same patrolman from the night before. A slightly more rumpled uniform. A little dirt on his boots. A definite edge of irritability in his voice. A vindictive gleam in his eyes. "Here I am, on my way to the station after a long night, and I see this blur of wedding gown fly by," he said. "And I think, what are the chances that's the same runaway bride I so gallantly tried to escort to the Methodist church just last night?" He looked at Sara with a sly smile. "And what do you know? It is the happy couple. Now, don't tell me you're still looking for the church."

"As a matter of fact, we are." Sara met his condescension with a haughty lift of her chin. "And it's very important that we aren't delayed."

"Really." He tapped the toe of his boot against the Harley's back tire. "Nice bike," he said to Ben. "Where'd you get it?"

"Tennessee."

"Bet it cost a penny or two."

"Three, actually."

The officer turned his humorless gaze to Sara in the sidecar, making her feel both anxious and annoyed at the same time. "What happened to the van you were driving the last time I stopped you? It was *your* van, wasn't it?"

She nodded impatiently. "It's mine, and there's something wrong with it."

"You don't say." The policeman shook his head in mock sympathy. "You mean something other than being stuck up to its fenders in what was once a beautiful lawn?"

Surprise slackened her jaw, but Sara rallied. "You . . . know about that?"

"Yeah. I got the call sometime after three o'clock this morning. It seems that one of Mr. Ridgeman's neighbors woke up to the sound of gently lapping waves...kind of like the ocean, you know. As it turns out, water from Mr. Ridgeman's busted sprinkler flooded his yard and filled up the drainage ditch, which then overflowed and flooded the neighbor's house." He chuckled. "I'm tellin' you, it's an unholy mess over there. Now, I can't tell you what to do, but

I will suggest that it wouldn't be a good idea to try to pick up your van today. Mr. Ridgeman was, uh... Let's just say, if you go anywhere near that house anytime soon, you'll be takin' your life into your own hands."

Her shoulders sagged. "I guess he's sort of angry."

The officer's lips curved. "Oh, yeah. I don't believe I've ever heard that kind of language spoken with such impact."

"Did he cuss?"

"Nope. He used a lot of big words that sounded seriously legal, though. I expect you'll be hearing from his lawyer real soon."

Her mouth went dry. "He is a lawyer."

The patrolman's eyebrows rose. "In that case, I'd advise you to put your affairs in order."

"It's been a pleasure talking with you, Officer," Ben said. "But we do have a wedding to get to, and we are in somewhat of a hurry."

"Uh-huh. Get out your papers for this vehicle. I'll just run the registration through the computer and make sure you didn't get somethin' for nothin'. If you know what I mean."

The line of Ben's jaw tightened, but he produced the necessary document. The patrolman took it and strolled to his car. Ben looked at her with a half smile. "I have a feeling this could take awhile."

"I guess I shouldn't have ducked away from his escort last night." She glanced back, knowing this delay could stretch on and on, tasting the bitter truth that West would never forgive her, that her plans for a future with him had drowned in one disastrous twinkle.

"Maybe if I offered to do community service, he'd let us go. I could teach driving school or something."

Ben's lips curved with a wry tenderness. "I'm not sure that would be considered community service. I suspect the delay will arise from the episode at Ridgeman's. The patrolman is probably checking to see if any charges are going to be filed."

"For damages, you mean."

"Don't worry about it. Ridgeman isn't going to sue you. You've seen him naked."

"That makes a difference?"

"Absolutely. Lawyers never want to be seen without their briefs." She rolled her eyes at his pun, and he grinned. "I learned that the first day of law school."

"I wish you hadn't dropped out. I have a feeling I'm going to need someone on my side."

He leaned toward her and touched the back of his hand to her cheek . . . and hurt her heart with his gentleness. "Sara, I'll be on your side until the last threads of my briefs unravel. And you can count on that."

"Thanks, Ben. You don't know how much I appreciate that, but at the moment, I'd rather count on getting a police escort to the church."

Surprise deepened the green of his eyes. "I suppose you're just going to sashay back there and explain to the officer that you're late and you require his assistance."

"Mostly just his siren." She handed the plastic-wrapped bridal gown to Ben. "At this point, I can't think of a thing I have to lose by asking." Pulling her skirt above her knees, she stepped out of the sidecar and headed for the patrol car.

"SARA! YOU'RE almost an hour late!" Mrs. Randolph, the mother of the bride, met her at the church doors. "Alicia is frantic! What were you doing in that police car? I thought the church was on fire when I heard the siren! I just know this is going to be a disaster. I told Alicia if you didn't show up she should call off the wedding. This isn't a good omen, you know."

Bridal gown in hand, Sara entered the church and soothed Mrs. Randolph with calm assurances that everything would be perfect. Just the way they'd planned. Everything was set up, the flowers in place, the tables decorated in the church's fellowship hall where a reception would take place after the ceremony. It was perfectly understandable that the mother of the bride would be concerned by the wedding coordinator's late arrival, but there was no need to worry. She had been unfortunately delayed by a slight misunderstanding with the policeman. But he had been persuaded to escort her to the church and she was here now. There was no point, Sara thought, in divulging how many hours she would be contributing to the annual fund-raiser for the policeman's auxiliary. A small price to pay for getting to the church on time, Ben had said before she was whisked away in the officer's speedy black-and-white patrol car, siren blaring, Ben following on the Harley.

When Sara entered the room where Alicia Randolph waited to change clothes, the bride-to-be took one look at the gown in Sara's hands and burst into nervous tears. "It's here," she said. "You brought it."

Sara thought if anyone had a right to a good dose of tears it would be her, and if she wasn't crying, no one else was going to, either. "Of course, I brought the dress," she said matter-of-factly as she pulled the plastic off the gown. "You didn't really think I wouldn't, did you?"

"Well, I..."

"No tears allowed. This is your wedding day, remember?"

Alicia smiled mistily. "It is, isn't it?"

"Yes, and it will be perfect." Sara began helping her into the wedding dress. "Trust me. I know what I'm doing."

FIVE HOURS LATER, Sara thought maybe there had been some basis for her confidence. The wedding ceremony had been perfect. The photography session relatively quick and painless. The reception at the church went as smoothly as possible, considering that it was not a catered affair and that the servers were all volunteers, by virtue of being somehow kin to the bride.

Rubbing a nagging ache in her left shoulder, Sara watched the bride and groom make their way past family and friends and a shower of birdseed. She wished she had been able to convince Alicia and her mother that a reception at a rented hall or a country club would have been much nicer. But they insisted on a one-stop wedding and reception at the church the family regularly attended. Now, Sara was left with the responsibility of putting the church back in order. An unaccustomed task and one she didn't relish.

It would take a half hour for the last of the guests to disperse. Another half hour before the bride's family finally walked out the door. For some reason, the mother of the bride seemed to think she needed to stay until the bitter end, making certain Sara didn't need further assistance. She had assured so many mothers, so many times, that she knew how to do her job, but it never seemed to make any difference.

As the solid, matronly Mrs. Randolph waved a final goodbye to her daughter, Sara braced for an onslaught of unnecessary reminders. An half hour later, she was still trying to hustle the woman out of the church.

"The groomsmen left their tuxedoes in the minister's study. You won't forget to return them to Mr. Formal Rentals, will you?" Mrs. Randolph scanned the sanctuary for an overlooked rose petal or one of the numerous Order of Ceremony bulletins that had littered the pews before Sara gathered them up. "And the candelabrum have to be at the florists no later than 10:00 a.m. Monday."

She acknowledged the information with a nod. "I'll make sure everything is returned on time and in good condition, Mrs. Randolph. Really, there is no need for you to worry."

"I know. You've handled everything beautifully. It's just hard...." A tear glistened in the mother's eye. "I'm going to miss her so much."

Sara commiserated with a weary smile and bit her tongue to keep from mentioning that, after a weeklong honeymoon, the new Mrs. Beggman would be living less than a mile away from her mother. "I'm sure it's difficult to let her go," she said instead. "But you must be very proud of her. She looked beautiful today."

That brought a smile through the tears. "She did, didn't she?"

"Yes. And you have a new son-in-law. Won't that be nice?"

The smile vanished. "He's a moron, no matter what Alicia says about him. But I won't go into that. I'm sure you could see for yourself what a total nincompoop he is."

"Mr. Randolph seems to like him."

"Mr. Randolph is also a moron." The woman sighed brusquely, as if she alone in all the world was surrounded by nincompoops. "I suppose I should go and find him. No telling where he's taken himself off to."

"I believe he's sitting outside in the car...waiting for you."

"You see what I mean? What sane person would sit in a hot car rather than stay inside where it's air-conditioned?"

Sara wanted to raise her hand, but she grasped Mrs. Randolph's elbow—lightly, but firmly—and walked with her to the door. "You go on home and relax," she said. "You can trust me to take care of everything here."

"All right, if you say so. I am a little tired." At last she stepped outside and Sara almost got the door closed. "Oh, Sara? I forgot to bring your check, but I'll put it in the mail first thing Monday morning."

With that bit of daunting information, the mother of the bride walked briskly across the parking lot to the car in which the nincompoop waited.

After locking the door, Sara checked the sanctuary one last time before she turned out the lights and hurried down a long hall to the large gathering room where the reception had been held.

Ben was nowhere to be seen, but he had obviously been here. The room had been returned to its original order. Chairs and tables were folded and stacked against a wall. The decorations were packed. The plates, silverware, cups and glasses she had borrowed from the church's kitchen were washed and put away. The tablecloths and napkins, also borrowed from the church as a substitute for the linens she had left in the van, were piled by the back door. She'd have them cleaned, of course, and return them later. Everything else was done.

Relief and gratitude blended into a smile—her first genuine smile since she'd arrived at the church. And Ben had put it there. Oh, sure, he'd probably gotten a few people to help him put away the tables and chairs. Most likely, a couple of those women who were fawning over him after he caught the bride's garter. But she didn't care. The wedding was over. She could go home and put her feet up... as soon as she found him.

"Ben?"

His name sounded hollow in the cavernous room and echoed slightly against the overhead beams.

"Ben?"

Had he left with those women? After declaring he'd stay with her until his underwear unraveled? The smile that tempted her lips was meant for her alone, but it curved upward for all to see... if there had been anyone left, that is. So where was Ben? And how was she going to get home?

The answer was parked outside the back door when she pushed it open and looked out. A shiny white van, nothing fancy, but still four wheels and a cargo space, awaited her like Cinderella's coach. The back was open and Ben was inside, loading the candelabrum. He jumped down and grinned at her. "Hi. I've almost got everything onboard . . . except for you, of course. The tables and chairs stay, right?"

She nodded. "How did you manage this?"

"I picked up one box and carried it out, then I went back and got another and carried it out. Then I—"

"The van," she interrupted. "How did you get the van?"

"I rented it."

"With an expired credit card?"

"It was a gold card, if you'll recall. I managed to pull a few strings and clear up the misunderstanding."

She wanted to believe him. "What kind of strings?"

"Will you stop worrying about that? It's all perfectly legal, I swear. I thought you'd be relieved, grateful even."

"I am, Ben, but . . . you're sure the policeman isn't going to come looking for us again?"

"After all the nonbillable hours you promised for his favorite charity? Not a chance. Trust me, Sara. This is a rental van and it isn't costing you a cent. Okay?"

There really was no reason to argue with him. However he'd gotten the van, she was more appreciative than she could say. "Thank you, Ben. How did you find the time to go get it?"

"I knew we couldn't move all this stuff with the Harley, so while you were busy telling the wedding party what to do and where to go and when, I slipped off. I got back just in time to catch the garter. Didn't you miss me?''

His thoughtfulness combined with the day's stress, and Sara did something she hadn't done since her seventeenth birthday, when she'd learned her mother hadn't died ten years before, but had simply walked away and never come back. She put her head in her hands and burst into tears.

Chapter Eleven

"You must think I'm an idiot, crying like that for no reason."

In the church's kitchen, Ben dabbed the corner of her eye with a wet paper towel and wiped away a smudge of mascara. "You just reached the end of your rope. Happens to all of us at one time or another." He blotted her other eye, pleased to have the excuse to keep her chin cupped in his hand. "If I'd remembered how susceptible you are to reverse psychology, though, I'd have done something mean instead."

"Do you do mean things, Ben?"

"My sister would tell you that the only person meaner than me is her ex-husband. But she's an idiot, so you can't believe what she says." His thumb made a slow, sensual stroke across her cheek, and Sara inhaled sharply, then released a low, shaky sigh.

"I'm okay," she said. "Really. I was just so surprised to walk into this room and discover all the work I thought I still had to do had already been done."

"You hired me to work, didn't you?"

"Well, yes, but normally, none of my employees would take the responsibility to pack a van, much less rent one."

"My motives were entirely selfish, I assure you. I didn't want those big candlesticks to scratch up my motorcycle."

She smiled, as if she knew the Harley had not been his main concern. "It's still the nicest thing that has happened to me in a long time."

He stopped dabbing, lifted her chin with a slight pressure and looked into her eyes. "In that case, your life is sadly deficient in nice things." Leaning forward, he brushed her lips with his, felt her shiver of response and returned for a deep and satisfying taste of her mouth.

It was several enjoyable seconds before Sara pulled away. "We're in the church," she whispered.

"I knew there was something holy about kissing you." He returned to her lips with an eager reverence and then proceeded to explore the line of her jaw with soft, swift nibbles.

She pulled away again, although he could tell that her resolve took longer to form and a good deal more effort to implement. "We should not be kissing in the church."

"Where should we be kissing?"

Her frown was barely worthy of the name. "Anywhere but here." She blinked, then stepped back with a shake of her head. "What am I saying? You and I should not be kissing at all."

"The earth didn't move for you?"

"Not even a tremor."

He tapped her chin with his fingertip. "Considering how conscious you are of being in a holy place, I'm surprised you'd tell such a whopper."

"Considering that I'm your employer, I'm surprised you'd call me a liar."

"You're feeling better, I can tell. Amazing what being caught in a lie can do for a person. It's as good at restoring the spirit as a dose of Vitamin C." He winked at her and turned away. "Let's get the rest of this paraphernalia loaded in the van. You and I have a date with destiny."

"You and I don't have a destiny. Not together, anyway." She followed him to the door, protesting, explaining. "Kissing in a church doesn't have any special significance, you know. And if I hadn't been feeling sort of, well, vulnerable..."

"It would have happened regardless, Sara. Now, you know that as well as I do." He pointed to one of the sacks full of linens. "You want to grab that? And I'll get these other two."

She picked up the sack and came after him through the doorway. "You're wrong about this, Ben."

"Look, if you can do a better job of packing the van, be my guest. I'm only trying to earn my keep. Frankly, I can't figure out how you got this amount of stuff to the church in the first place."

"It took several trips during the week, and I have to return a lot of things that were delivered by someone else." She handed him the sack she carried. "And that isn't what I was talking about. I don't want you to think we have a future together, because we don't."

Ben held the sack in his arms for a moment, letting her denial wither from lack of agreement, then he shrugged complacently and turned his attention to the van.

"It is ludicrous even to talk about it."

He didn't answer, and her frustration thickened the air between them.

"I hardly know you, for Pete's sake."

"I distinctly remember hearing you say that you could tell everything you needed to know about me from a single glance. Has that famous intuition of yours suffered a breakdown since last night?" He put a hand on each of her shoulders and moved her back a step. Then, with a smile, he headed inside the church.

She stayed right on his heels. "That was different."

"Was it?"

"Don't mess with me, Ben. You know it was."

"Why? Because you say so?" He picked up the last box and balanced it in his arms. "Because you didn't *plan* to fall in love with me?"

That stopped her cold. He had the box loaded and was closing the cargo doors when she came up with an answer.

"You are delusional, Mr. Northcross."

He laughed, thoroughly in love with his destiny. "Probably, Ms. Gunnerson. But that doesn't change the facts. You and I still have a date with—"

"Not in this lifetime."

"—the twinkling wedding dress—"

"That's not destiny."

"—dinner at your house—"

"Canceled."

"—and an appointment to meet your new neighbor... not necessarily in that order." If he had taken a damp towel and washed her face, he couldn't have done better at wiping the argument from her expression.

"The baby," she said, as if she'd only just remembered. "I wonder if she's had the baby."

Ben jerked his head toward the church. "Lock up and we'll go to the hospital to find out. If you can tell me how to get there from here, that is."

"I'll drive. You lock up." She grabbed the keys from his hand, tossed him the church keys, and headed for the driver's seat, confidence restored, purpose renewed, completely in charge again.

"DEENEE? SARA." Pressing her finger against her ear, Sara turned away from the noise around her and spoke directly into the mouthpiece of the phone. "Can you do something for me? A favor?"

There was a slight hesitation. "Does it involve my brother?"

"No. Well, not directly."

"Oh, Sara, I really don't want to go anywhere near West. He's still foaming at the mouth."

Sara sighed. "I suppose it will be awhile before he's in the mood to forgive and forget."

"I'd say Christmas, the year 2001, at the earliest. West holds a grudge longer than anyone else in the world. Maybe longer. You're not calling to ask me to play peacemaker, are you?"

"No," Sara said quickly. "Of course not. I just . . . left something at his house and I need it."

"And you thought you could talk me into going and getting it for you, right?"

"I wouldn't ask, except I have to have the wedding dress. Ben can't leave without it."

"The wedding dress?" DeeNee's voice picked up interest. "The one you had on last night?"

"That would be the one, yes. I left it under Arthur's bed."

"You're sure?"

"What kind of question is that? I should know where I left it."

"And you want me to go over there and get it?"

"Well, yes, if you could. I can pick it up later or I'll meet you somewhere in the morning. I just don't know how soon I'll be able to leave the hospital, so I can't give you an exact time. But if you'll do this for me, I'll—"

"Hospital? What are you doing at the hospital?"

"Waiting for a baby."

"Last night you didn't even want a dog."

"My neighbor is having the baby. I'm just here to provide moral support."

"Okay, I'll wrangle the dress from Arthur and then I'll keep it here at my house until I hear from you. Is that all right?"

"Perfect. You don't know how much I appreciate this, DeeNee."

"Yes, I do."

"I'll do you a favor in return someday."

"You better believe you will."

"SO I LIED." Ben placed three white paper sacks on the table in Sara's kitchen. "I would have cooked a spectacular dinner for you if the little tadpole hadn't waited until one o'clock in the morning to make his appearance. Marcy's Twenty-Four Hour Chinese Take-Out is the best I could do under the circumstances." He pulled back a chair. "Sit."

Sara sat.

He put a sack in front of her. "Eat."

She looked up. "Would you mind if I take off my shoes first?"

"Take off anything you like." He sat across from her and opened one of the sacks. He removed a carton imprinted with Chinese lettering, then two sets of chopsticks. He put one to Sara's right on the table.

She slipped off her shoes and rubbed the back of her calf with the other foot as she picked up the chopsticks and opened her sack. Her stomach cramped with anticipation at the mouthwatering smells emanating from inside.

"Mmm." She uttered a contented murmur half a carton later.

"Mmm." Ben answered with the same appreciation.

They reached for the same egg roll at the same moment, and her fingertips slid across the back of his hand, encountering a texture as tantalizing as the downy feel of the blanket wrapped around Gypsy's baby. Ben's gaze held hers for a breathless moment as his words echoed in her memory. *Didn't plan to fall in love... didn't plan didn't plan...*

"You take it." She drew back her hand. "I think there's one in this other sack." Concentrating on finding another egg roll, she pretended it was just the same to be alone in her kitchen with Ben, sharing cartons of Chinese food, as it would have been with Jason or Gypsy or practically anyone else. As long as she didn't notice the seductive slant of his smile, the unabashed desire in his eyes, it was exactly the same. Comfortable, companionable, congenial. All she had to do was keep her hands off his egg roll.

"Have you ever held a newborn before?" she asked as if she'd been thinking about the baby all along. "I had no idea what to do with him."

"Gypsy and Kevin seem to have gotten the hang of it rather quickly."

"I don't suppose they have a choice."

"When my niece was born, I was the first one, other than her mother, to hold her. I remember thinking if I didn't hold her tightly I would drop her, but if I held her too tightly I would suffocate her. It was the most responsibility I've ever held in my hands."

Sara agreed with a nod as she wiped each finger in turn. "And then, on top of having to learn what to do with the baby, you have to come up with a name for it. And whatever you choose, the kid is stuck with it for the rest of his life."

"You can stop worrying about that. Gypsy is not going to name her baby Tadpole."

"She says she is."

"Uh-huh. Well, my intuition tells me he'll have a nice, conventional name like his father. He may even be Kevin, Jr."

"Not in a million years."

"Want to wager on the possibility?" He glanced at the sacks, cartons, napkins, rice and scattered drops of soy sauce on the table. "Whoever wins has to clean up."

"Since they haven't decided on a name, this table might not get cleaned for days. Besides, I know I'm right, and much as I'd like to take advantage of you, it wouldn't be fair."

He leaned toward her, his dark green eyes involving hers in a seductive gaze. "Take advantage of me," he said. "I dare you."

Exactly what he was daring her to do, she couldn't be sure. But there was no doubt what tempting images cavorted through her thoughts—erotic vignettes of Ben sweeping her off her feet and into his arms, carrying her to her bedroom, removing her dress one sensual inch at a time, leaving the imprint of his lips wherever the dress had touched. Sara stood so fast her chair rocked backward and nearly fell. "I'll clean up," she said quickly. "You take Cleo out."

"She's already been out." Ben stood, too, and the room suddenly seemed to contract into a much smaller space, as if his size, his presence, his sheer masculinity couldn't be contained in this one place. Or maybe the kitchen just wasn't big enough for the two of them and her runaway imagination.

"I'll take her out again." Sara headed for the living room, escape from her totally unsuitable fantasies uppermost on her agenda.

Cleo was snoozing, draped like a rag doll in the arms of the overstuffed chair.

"Cleo." Sara clapped her hands. "Want to go for a walk?"

The Lab opened one eye and promptly closed it again.

"Come on, girl. Don't you need to stretch your legs?"

This time, she yawned and tucked her nose in the crevice between the chair's upholstered arm and the seat cushion.

Feeling a little desperate, Sara tried shaking the dog awake. "Cleo, wake up. Let's go outside." And received a leave-me-be growl for her effort.

"I don't think she's in the mood," Ben said from the doorway.

"Nonsense. Dogs love the outdoors."

"She loves that chair at the moment." The corners of his mouth tipped with a wry smile as he leaned— quite attractively—against the door frame. "If you want to take a walk, though, go ahead. You don't need to use Cleo as an excuse."

"I just thought she would want—"

"You just thought that taking her out would be a way to save face and escape temptation at the same time."

Sara widened her eyes in an attempt to look indignant. "Is that your intuition at work again, Ben? Because, frankly, I had nothing more on my mind than the dog's comfort."

He looked at Cleo, sprawled unladylike across the armchair. "If she gets any more comfortable, she'll become a permanent part of that chair." He turned his gaze to Sara. "And even my intuition is no match for you when it comes to what you do or don't have on your mind."

Breathing was becoming a struggle, because even if he truly had no idea what was on her mind, she had no such luxury. Her imagination, aided by very real bits of memory, invoked visions of long, wet kisses and slow, sensual touches, Ben without a shirt and her without . . .

"Look, Ben, I'm going to bed."

His lazy smile ambled into place. "Either you're inviting me to join you or you're issuing a hell of a challenge."

"Is everything a contest to you? I made a simple statement. I'm going to bed. I didn't say will you join me. And I certainly didn't say don't try to stop me. There. Now is my intention clear?"

The smile developed a roguish slant. "As clear as if I could read your mind." He straightened and walked toward her. "But Sara . . ."

It took all her willpower not to retreat before his advance.

"Maybe it's time I made my intentions clear to you." He stopped in front of her and gathered one of her hands in each of his.

Too late for retreat, she thought. Any more brilliant strategic moves on her part and she'd be at checkmate. "Not necessary, Ben. Really. This is not—"

"Oh, but it is. Because I want you to understand that I intend to marry you."

She gulped and tried to say something, anything, but her voice had deserted her. And Ben, damn it, took advantage of her incoherence and kissed her. A long, wet, debilitating kiss that she should have stopped, *would* have stopped if she'd been thinking clearly. If he hadn't tasted of Chinese spices and lusty temptations. If his arms hadn't gathered her against him in a light but compelling embrace. If she hadn't felt blissfully, wonderfully right about participating in this exercise of mutual attraction.

Didn't plan to fall in love... didn't plan...

If she had an ounce of willpower, she'd inform Ben that this was lust, pure and simple. Of course, she hadn't planned on falling into lust, either. But there was not much point in denying that's exactly what she was in. And as long as he kept kissing her, kept her wrapped in his arms and entwined in this fantasy-laden state of mind, it didn't make much difference whether she called it lust or love. At the moment, the two felt remarkably the same.

"Hey."

Jason came in through the front door and Sara pulled guiltily away from Ben, blinking furiously to bring her brother into focus. "Hey," she repeated in a voice two sizes too thick.

"Don't mind me." Hardly sparing a glance, Jason moved down the hall with a fast stride and a sure purpose. "I just came to get a few of my CDs."

Sara avoided looking at Ben and hoped he wouldn't notice how disconcerted she was by the interruption. "You're not going out again," she called down the hall. "Not at this hour."

Jason breezed through the living room on his way to the door. "I'm nineteen, Sis. I don't need permission to stay out all night and listen to music with my friends."

"But you could get into trouble," she protested.

Jason paused in the doorway to look from her to Ben and then back to her. "Yeah," he said. "And with any luck, so could you. See ya tomorrow." And with that, he was gone.

She stared at the closed door, fighting the impulse to walk right over to Ben and take up exactly where they left off. But that would be asking for trouble. And Lord knows, she didn't need . . .

The next thing she knew, Ben's arms were around her, her chin was lifting, her pulse racing, the urgency sweeping over her like a summer storm as his lips made a slow descent to meet hers. She could only speculate about which one of them had made the first move, but there was no doubt she had met him halfway. Ever since she'd set eyes on that antique wedding gown, she hadn't been herself. All her plans had been turned upside down in one little twinkle. Impulses had become second nature. Sane, careful planning had given way to insane, reckless actions.

Not that she felt particularly insane or reckless right now. Her arms were wound around Ben's neck, and she twined her fingers in the thickness of his hair. In fact, she felt particularly rational at the moment. She was tired of being cautious, weary of keeping her emotions in check and exhausted from planning for the future.

Her plans and her future had evaporated before her eyes, all because of one silly impulse. What difference would it make if she gave in to one more? Tomorrow Ben would be on his way, with his dog and the antique bridal gown. There wouldn't be room for her, even if she wanted to go with him, even if he remembered that tonight he'd intended to marry her.

She knew his talk about love and forever was as much an illusion as the twinkle of a wedding dress. But at the moment, it seemed real and within her reach. So what if it vanished at sunup? So what if Ben was every man who had ever stolen her heart? What did she have left to lose by believing his love was meant for her alone, that a commitment made at first glance could last forever, that there were sometimes moments of magic that couldn't be explained away?

Ben sensed a change in her attitude. Actually, he would have had to be completely insensitive not to notice the caress of her hands in his hair, the repositioning of her body against his, the subtle—possibly unintentional, but highly suggestive—movement of her hips. Until then, he had fully intended to let the kiss wear itself out and conclude this phase of seduction by sending Sara to bed alone. He hadn't really considered pressing her for more. And now, suddenly, he found himself hard-pressed—in more ways than one—to know how he was supposed to respond.

He drew back. Well, at least, he tried to draw back. But in a surprise attack, she moved with him, maintaining full body contact and throwing his balance off. He grabbed her to keep from falling, but it was too late—or else she pushed him—and he tumbled backward, striking the backs of his knees on the edge of the sofa and sprawling inelegantly across the cushions.

If Sara noticed his groping efforts to pull himself, and her, into a more comfortable position, she gave no sign. Her kiss was relentless. Her body issued every invitation known to man. She had gone from escape to capitulation in zero point one seconds, and Ben knew that if he lived to be a hundred and twenty, he would never meet anyone like her. This was his once-in-a-lifetime, the surprise he'd been searching for as long as he could remember. She was his destiny as surely as he was hers, and since there was no glory in struggling against the inevitable, he settled back to let her seduce him.

As if he could have stopped her.

Sara slipped her hand inside his shirt, excited by the discovery that she liked taking the initiative. She liked the way his breathing escalated when she touched his chest just so. She liked the feel of his hair-roughened skin and the muscular proportions of his chest. She liked the pull of desire deep inside her when his kisses trailed from her chin to her ear and down to the hollows of her neck. But most of all, she liked the scary but exhilarating sensation of being out of control, of not taking responsibility beyond this moment, of letting this impulse take her where it would.

Her fingertips tousled the thick hair at his nape. He tensed at the touch, and the reaction pleased her. She had never felt overly confident when it came to sex. She could count her experiences on one hand...with a few fingers to spare. Obviously, she needed to let her ambition take over this phase of her life, too. Take control. Insist that she be the one to set the pace and guide his responses, instead of the other way around.

Ben took her bottom lip in his mouth and sucked gently, stripping her willpower to naked desire and making her think that maybe it was all right for him to be the guide every now and then. There was no need to be selfish, and geez, he was so *good* with his lips.

Apparently, he knew how to use his hands, too. His fingertips traced a delicate blueprint of longing from the base of her neck to the base of her spine, and Sara trembled as she imagined how it would feel without a layer of clothing separating her from him.

His slow, sultry kisses raised her blood pressure and promised the discovery of pleasures she hadn't dreamed lay hidden within her, like a vein of gold waiting to be mined. He branded her throat, her cheeks, then returned to her mouth for a long, wet, soul-searing kiss. She lay passive and pliable, half on, half off his flat stomach, while his long fingers climbed her ribs until he could cup one of her breasts in his palm.

So, okay, he was a better guide than she was. He obviously had an itinerary all his own, and while she wasn't entirely thrilled at being relegated to follow his lead, she recognized that there were some advantages. For one, she could simply enjoy the scents, the sounds and the sensations of his efforts. For another, she didn't have to bear the responsibility for making a single decision. She had meant to take charge, but he was in full command. She had meant to tease, but his irrefutable demands required her serious attention. What she had imagined as a languorous escape from reality he transformed into a passionate contest with possession of her heart as the prize he meant to claim.

"Sara," he whispered tenderly into her ear. "I've waited all my life to hold you like this."

She braced her weight on her hands and frowned at him, mostly because he'd stopped kissing and started talking. "We just met."

"Very romantic," he said with a sigh. "And I'm trying so hard to sweep you off your feet."

"Too late. I tripped you up first."

"Several times." He kissed the tip of her nose. "Would I be overstepping the limits of your hospitality if I suggested we continue this discussion in your bedroom?''

"Something wrong with my couch?''

"No. I was trying to be sensitive to Cleo's feelings. Her self-esteem may be shattered by all the attention I'm giving you.''

Cleo's snore was timely and conclusive.

Ben shrugged. "Okay, so I thought you'd be more comfortable if you had a little more space to move about.''

"As long as you're kissing me, comfort isn't high among my priorities.''

His smile held the pleasure of all the kisses they'd shared. "I'm planning to take this a little further than kissing... if you agree, of course.''

"I shouldn't, you know.'' Their eyes met, sharing the knowledge that they had passed the point of agreement some time back. "Any man who says he intends to marry a woman in order to seduce her doesn't deserve to spend the night in her arms.''

"If seduction was my only objective, I would have simply said I'll respect you in the morning and made my life easier.''

Thoughts of West intruded... and were ridiculously easy to get rid of. All she had to do was lower her mouth to Ben's and skirt the corner of his lips with her tongue. He groaned, and her feeling of power asserted itself again. She pushed to her feet, took a firm grip on his hand and pulled him upright.

The journey down the hallway was interrupted several times while Ben tested her agreement with another round of beguiling kisses. She pressed his back against the wall while she reached around him and switched off the bedroom light Jason had left on. The next stop was at Ben's insistence, and Sara leaned against the door of the bathroom as his lips trailed down her throat and his hands kneaded the firmness of her breasts. She was breathless with yearning when he drew back to ask, "Do you have protection?"

Barely able to keep from melting at his feet, she nodded at the medicine chest. Ben opened the mirrored chest and whistled in surprise. "I realize you like to plan ahead, Sara, but..."

She looked past him at the boxes of condoms stacked one on top of another on every shelf. "My nineteen-year-old brother lives here, too."

"This seems optimistic, even for a teenager."

"He doesn't buy them. I do. I figure it betters the odds that he'll at least stop and think before he tumbles head over heels into trouble."

"Does it work for you, too?"

"You forget how susceptible I am to reverse psychology."

"I wasn't going to mention that."

She sighed. "To be honest, this is the first time the question has come up."

He approached her, stepping within her space, lifting his hands to cup her face. "I recently heard someone say that anticipation is half the pleasure."

"If you're trying to take my mind off the disaster I've made of my life, repeating what you overheard in West's bedroom is not the way to go about it."

"You're about to forget any other man exists." He leaned closer, and she trembled with anticipation. "I give you my personal guarantee." He switched off the light, and then his lips covered hers with forgetfulness.

By the time they reached the bedroom, her dress was unbuttoned to the waist and her bra pushed aside by his eager hands. He had lost his shirt outside the doorway and claimed her breasts as compensation. When they fell together across the bed, lips, arms and legs all entangled, Sara wondered when he'd finished unbuttoning the dress and how he'd gotten it off without her noticing.

Not that it mattered. If he hadn't gotten rid of it, she would have. But she did wish she had the same finesse in getting rid of his clothes. It took awhile, and required judicious amounts of his help, but eventually he had on fewer articles of clothing than she did. A fact he remedied without delay before proceeding with the luxurious task of disarming her impatience with slow, wet kisses and singular, seductive strokes of his fingertips on her skin.

Her senses swam with new sensations, her blood pounded like crashing surf in her veins, her heart strained with her body to be closer, to lose herself in his touch and to claim a corner of his memory for all time. She wouldn't forget him anytime soon, and she meant to make sure he didn't forget her, either.

As his mouth returned to hers, his body covered her and she trembled, anticipating the aching pleasure of belonging in his arms. It was the safest place she had ever been. And the scariest. But she wouldn't think about tomorrow. She wouldn't feel past this moment, this specific *now*. When Ben belonged, heart and soul, to her.

Chapter Twelve

The phone kept ringing. Sara pulled a pillow over her head and waited for the incessant noise to stop. When it didn't, she lifted the edge of the pillow and peeped at the clock on her bedside table. Not even six o'clock yet. Someone had a sick sense of humor.

A husky sigh came from the other side of the bed. Easing a foot beneath the covers, she first encountered Ben's warmth and then his long, hairy leg. His arm slid over her shoulder, and he draped himself around her. For a moment, Sara lay still, remembering the passionate energy they had created in this bed only a few hours earlier. She snuggled against him, wondering how that energy had become this safe, lazy serenity. His breath stirred strands of hair at the base of her neck, and she let the pillow slide to the floor while she savored the experience of waking up next to Ben.

At least, she intended to savor it, if the phone ever stopped ringing.

"Take it off the hook." He whispered the temptation, making it seem not only enticing, but essential.

She groped for the phone and dragged the receiver to her ear. "You have the wrong number," she mumbled and was just about to drop the receiver on the floor when she heard a far-off and distressed, "Sara!"

Cupping the phone against her ear, she heard a panicked voice, "Sara! Don't hang up! Are you there?"

"DeeNee?"

"Yes. Listen, last night when you said you'd do something for me in return? Well, now's the time. I need a favor and I need it now."

"Now?"

Behind her, Ben made a husky protest.

"It's important, Sara. You've got to get me out of this dress."

"Dress?" Sara frowned. "What dress?"

"The wedding gown. I'm in it and I can't get out."

"Where are you?"

"At West's house. Locked in Arthur's room."

"What are you doing there?"

"I came to get the dress for you and the next thing I knew, I had it on. Please get over here as quick as you can."

"You're wearing the wedding dress?"

"Yes, and it didn't even twinkle at me, either. Will you come?"

"Of course. I'll be there as quickly as possible."

DeeNee's relief echoed over the phone line. "One more thing. You have to kidnap Harry Schaffer and bring him with you."

Before Sara could blink, the phone clicked and she was left contemplating the wrong end of a bizarre conversation.

"Do you know this guy?" Ben asked as Sara rang the doorbell.

"We've met."

"I've met Dustin Hoffman. That doesn't mean I know him well enough to ring his doorbell at seven in the morning."

She stopped checking the meticulous lettering over the brass mailbox outside Harry Schaffer's apartment and turned to look at him. "You've met Dustin Hoffman?"

"On a movie set."

Tipping her head to the side, she smiled and all but charmed his socks off. "You surprise me sometimes, Ben."

"You surprise me constantly, Sara."

She gave the doorbell another push. "Come on, Harry," she said. "DeeNee made this sound like a matter of life and death."

The dead bolt clicked and the door opened. Short, balding and eagle-eyed, Harry Schaffer looked from Ben to Sara with ill-disguised impatience and said nothing.

"Hi," Sara said. "This is Ben. I'm Sara. We met at West Ridgeman's house the other night?"

The impatience didn't alter. Neither did the silence.

"There's been a slight, uh, misunderstanding," Sara said. "At least I think I must have misunderstood." She glanced at Ben. "Actually, DeeNee called and asked us to come by here and pick you up. She said you were the only one who could straighten things out."

"DeeNee Ridgeman?"

"That's right."

"DeeNee," he repeated, and Ben decided Schaffer was probably a heck of an attorney. He certainly had the poker face down pat. "Why would DeeNee Ridgeman ask you to pick me up?"

"She didn't tell me, but it sounded urgent." Sara smiled, and Ben didn't see how Schaffer could resist.

"You're positive she asked for me?" Harry looked past them at the empty sidewalk. "Specifically?"

"Oh, yes." Sara nodded vigorously. "She was very specific."

"She wants me to straighten things out," he said, almost to himself. "What kind of things?"

"We don't know," Ben answered, taking the initiative. "But she definitely thinks you can fix whatever it is."

He appeared flattered, but it was hard to tell for sure. "Where is she?"

"Waiting for you. Shall we go?"

"Go where?"

Sara frowned. "Do you always ask so many questions?"

"Usually more."

Ben leaned against the wall, crossed his arms and observed the exchange with interest. Hard to believe that only hours before he had been seduced by this woman. He hoped it would happen again, too, and not so many hours from now, either.

"She's at West's house. Do you want to ride with us in the van or take your own car?" Sara nodded encouragement. "Your choice."

"Why didn't she call me herself?" Harry asked. "Why did she send you?"

"I don't know," Sara replied. "Maybe she thought you wouldn't come if she asked."

"But she must be aware of how I feel...." He stopped. "I'll go."

"We'll take you."

Harry stepped outside and closed the door, obviously not caring that he was wearing a bathrobe and slippers. "I'm ready."

Ben looked at Sara and shrugged as the three of them headed for the van.

HARRY SAT FORWARD in his seat and stared as Sara drove through the open gates onto West's property. On the way up the driveway, they passed three trucks from Green Toes Lawn Service, two vans from Secure Security, two utility trucks from the electric company and a station wagon with a magnetic sign on the door that read Boots Plumbing. Sara did a few simple calculations in her head, adding the number of trucks, multiplying the number of workers, and hoped they weren't getting paid double overtime for working on the weekend. Even without figuring that in, she had to wince at the total.

"What happened here?" Harry asked. "This looks like a garden party, except there doesn't seem to be a garden."

"Or a lawn." Ben checked the progress of the repairs. "Looks like they're going to put in a whole new system."

"Hmm," Harry said. "I thought West just installed this one a couple of months ago."

"Probably wasn't working right," Ben said nonchalantly.

"That seems odd."

"West is very particular about his lawn, you know." Sara kept her voice even and unconcerned, although her stomach was doing an anxious loop-de-loop as she steered around the pile of dirt and timbers that once had been a rose garden. "We're here."

Arthur opened the kitchen door for them. "Well, well. Returning to the scene of the crime, are we?" He nodded to Harry. "Good morning, Mr. Schaffer. You're a little late for the pajama party. Perhaps you're here to have breakfast with Mr. West?"

"He's here at DeeNee's request." Sara wanted to get in and out before West found out she had been there. "This way, Harry."

"My job offer still stands, Arthur," Ben said, following Sara and Harry Schaffer up the stairs. "You can work for me anytime you say."

"How comforting." Arthur came up the steps after them. "I do hope Miss DeeNee didn't invite the three of you to join her for breakfast in my bedroom."

"She said she was locked in." Sara looked at the butler accusingly. "And since you have a master key..."

Arthur's eyebrows rose in offended dignity. "Miss DeeNee locked herself inside my room, with my keys, and has refused to come out."

"You don't have an extra key?" Harry asked in a Perry Mason kind of voice. "That's odd."

"It's my room, Mr. Schaffer," Arthur said. "For privacy reasons, there is only one key. Until recently—" he glanced pointedly at Sara "—that hasn't been a problem."

Ben leaned toward the closed door and rapped his knuckles on the wood. "Rapunzel, Rapunzel, open the door. Prince Charming is here."

Harry shifted from one slippered foot to the other. "I don't understand why she wanted me to—"

The door flew open, and in an instant, Harry Schaffer lost whatever he had meant to say, his implacable calm and his poker face. He stood outside Arthur's bedroom, awestruck at the sight of DeeNee Ridgeman in the wedding dress.

She stared back, equally fascinated by Harry Schaffer in his bathrobe.

"DeeNee," he said.

"Harry," she replied.

"You look incredible."

"So do you." Her smile seemed a little nervous. "I can't seem to get this dress unbuttoned. Do you think you..."

"It will be my pleasure." He stepped into the room, and the door swung shut.

Ben looked at Sara. "I think they want to be alone."

"In my bedroom?" Arthur, for once, appeared confused.

"It certainly looks that way," Ben said, turning toward the stairs. "I'm going to rustle up some grub. Anyone want to join me?"

Sara turned to Arthur with a frown. "Did she ask you to unbutton the dress?"

"Yes, but she wouldn't hold still, kept walking back and forth in front of the mirror." Arthur stared at the closed door. "When it became obvious she couldn't get out of the dress, I went to get the scissors. That's when she locked herself in."

"Does West know about this?"

The butler continued to frown at his bedroom door. "He has had a couple of restless nights and isn't awake yet this morning."

"Restless nights, huh?" Ben paused on his way to the kitchen. "Wonder why. He must have lost an important case recently."

"I don't lose important cases." West's voice traveled up the stairs, snapping everyone to attention. "Arthur? What's going on up there? Who are you talking to?"

Arthur looked at Sara and lifted his thin shoulders in a small apology before he answered. "Ms. Gunnerson," he said. "And Ben, the bartender from the other evening."

"Sara?" West questioned the information. "Sara's here?" The stairs creaked as he started up them.

Swallowing hard, Sara prepared a whole slew of apologies in case West put her on trial here and now. "Hi, West," she said as he stopped and stared at her from one stair below where Ben continued to stand. "You're probably surprised to see me this morning, aren't you?"

"Nothing you do surprises me, Sara." His gaze turned to take Ben's measure. "It's a trifle early in the day for a glass of wine, but unless you're here to pour one for me, I can't imagine what you're doing in my house."

"I'm not a bartender today," Ben said evenly. "I'm here to pick up a wedding dress."

"You're obviously in the wrong place at the wrong time, because there isn't a wedding dress within a mile radius."

A muffled giggle could be heard behind the closed door, and West's attention swung in that direction. "Who is in there?"

No one answered, and he pinned Sara with a demanding gaze. "Will you please explain who is in there and what is going on?"

She wished he wouldn't use that tone of voice. And she wished Ben wouldn't keep leaning against the stairwell with his arms crossed, looking from her to West as if he had a secret he couldn't wait to share. And she wished DeeNee had taken the dress home with her before she tried it on. And she wished she had Ben's camouflage pants and vest so she could just blend into her surroundings and no one would know she was here.

On second thought, she wished she wasn't here. "DeeNee needed help," she began hesitantly. "And I owed her a favor and—"

"My sister's in there?" West pointed at Arthur's bedroom door.

Sara nodded, feeling guilty despite having nothing to do with whatever was happening behind that closed door. "With Harry Schaffer."

"What?" West pushed past Ben to get to the door and pounded his fist against it. "DeeNee, if you're in there, you'd better get out here this minute."

"Go away, West. You bother me." A giggle followed, and he pounded on the door again.

"Don't make me come in there after you, DeeNee. Think about what you're doing. Think about who you're—"

The door opened and Harry stepped out, tightening the sash on his rumpled bathrobe. "I'm going to marry your sister, Ridgeman," he said. "Get used to calling me brother."

West looked stunned, then angry as he shoved the door back on its hinges. "DeeNee? What in hell is going on around here?"

"Good morning, West." DeeNee, clad only in an oversize T-shirt, walked to her brother and kissed him on the cheek. "Congratulate me. Harry and I are engaged."

"This is rather sudden, isn't it? I wasn't aware the two of you were dating."

"It happened very suddenly." DeeNee smiled at her fiancé, and he smiled back. "And we have Sara and Ben to thank for it."

Sara blinked. Even Ben looked surprised.

"And what," West asked, "did they have to do with your engagement?"

"Well, if Sara hadn't put on the wedding dress, I might never have thought of trying this. Ben was the only person who could unbutton the dress when she was wearing it, you see. And I had this idea that if I put on the dress, Harry would have to be the one to unbutton me."

"You're talking nonsense," West said sternly. "What wedding dress? And why would Sara be wearing it?"

DeeNee pointed at the bed, where the wedding dress lay in ivory innocence. "That's the dress, and she wore it over here Friday night because Ben's dog ate the other dress."

His gaze turned like clockwork to Sara.

"It's a long story," she said. "And really it isn't all that interesting." He obviously wasn't satisfied with that answer, so she tried again. "That dress ended up at my house by accident and it . . . I accidentally put it on and then I couldn't get it off and the dog tore the dress I meant to wear to the party and . . . and Ben did have to unbutton the dress for me."

West stroked his chin. "Let me be sure I understand. You *accidentally* put on a wedding dress and wore it to my house?"

Her eyes caught the glint of amusement in Ben's eyes, but she didn't feel much like laughing as she answered West with a halting nod.

To her surprise, West was the one who laughed. "That is priceless, Sara. Absolutely priceless. Tell me, did this *accident* happen before or after you *accidentally* relandscaped my yard?"

"That was an accident, West. You can't think I would damage your property on purpose."

His lips formed a smug reply. "You do have considerable manipulative skills, Sara. This wouldn't be the first time you've done something to get my attention."

"You think I *planned* to tear out your sprinkler system?"

"Perhaps not specifically, but you have to admit that if you wanted me to take over your business, being in my debt would be one way to facilitate that. And, although I don't have a final figure, you are going to owe me a great deal of money."

She was stunned. "Why would you think I'd want you to own my business?"

"Perhaps we should continue this discussion in private." He reached for her hand, motioned DeeNee into the hall, then pulled Sara inside Arthur's bedroom. After closing the door, he raised her chin with the tip of his finger. "Hasn't your master plan been to marry me since the first day we met?"

She was too embarrassed to admit that she'd planned their first meeting, as well, so she nodded a reluctant agreement.

"So, when we became husband and wife, then my investment in your business would be a given, anyway. I believe you were just hoping to speed up the process. Tell me, sweetness, when you put on the wedding gown, did you plan on accidentally getting me in front of a minister? Or were you hoping that once I saw you in bridal white, I'd drop to my knee and propose?"

Sara didn't need his help to lift her chin another degree. "No, West. That wasn't my intention at all. It was all the result of one rather silly impulse. An accident."

He chuckled softly. "You're not impulsive, Sara. And you don't do anything by accident. That's one of the things I love about you. You're so predictable." His knuckles stroked softly across her cheek as his voice lowered to a whisper meant only for her ears. "Even the other night... I was surprised to find you in my room, but I wasn't surprised to find you were gone when I got out of the shower. You're not a seductress, Sara. You're an intelligent, ambitious woman and you don't have to stage a disaster or put on an ugly old wedding dress to convince me to marry you. I decided two weeks ago that I would ask you to be my wife. I had planned on a more romantic place and time, but you're obviously impatient, so..." He held her hand and got down on one knee, and Sara wished more than anything that he'd get up and not say what he was about to say.

But he said it. He proposed marriage, offered her the security of his name, his position, the stability of his home and family. This was the future she had planned for herself, the reality she had shaped with her own actions, the destiny she had manufactured from her own design. How could she refuse it? Why would she even consider doing so?

Because Ben had a laugh that made her happy? Because his touch made her shiver with desire? Because he was all the risks she dared not take in one enticing package?

And that, of course, was her answer. Ben was a risk. He hadn't asked her to marry him and wasn't going to. He might spend a week with her, or a year, talking about love and marriage and the future, but sooner or later, he'd lose interest and move on. And no amount of planning on her part would stop him.

"Sara?" West was still on his knee, still waiting for her answer. "Say you'll marry me before my leg cramps, okay?"

She looked at the wedding dress on the bed. The ugly old dress that had brought Ben into her life, and would take him out of it, as well. It was just a dress. She could see that now. It hadn't twinkled. It wasn't magic. It was just an old, ugly dress. With a sigh, she shut out the memory of Ben's kisses and gave West her predictable, unsurprising, "Yes."

BEN STUFFED his backpack into the sidecar and then carefully folded the plastic-wrapped wedding gown on top of it. He covered the cargo with Cleo's blanket and patted it down to make a nest for her. But eventually, of course, there was nothing left to do except leave.

He looked at the house where Sara lived and said goodbye to a porch swing and kids playing in the yard. They'd never really existed, anyway. He'd been foolish to imagine he could ever be part of such a scene.

The front door opened and Sara stepped onto the porch. Across the yard, their eyes met and Ben looked away first. His heart ached with love for her, its rhythm so heavy he couldn't understand how it could keep beating. Until she and West had walked, hand in hand, out of Arthur's bedroom that morning and announced their engagement, it hadn't occurred to Ben that she might not return his love or that her heart might choose someone else. Until that moment, he hadn't realized he could lose.

She approached the Harley with measured steps and with Cleo at her side. "Sure you won't stay for lunch?" she asked brightly.

"I can't, but thanks, anyway." He patted the blanket, smoothing it out, tucking in the corners, pretending he was anxious to be on the road. "It's been great, but..."

"Adventure calls. I know." She leaned down and scratched Cleo's ear. "You're invited to the wedding... if you're in the neighborhood."

He'd rather carve his heart into ribbons with a butter knife. "I doubt I'll be back this way anytime soon."

She nodded as if she'd expected that answer. "I thought maybe I should explain about this morning... about the engagement."

"What's to explain? You told me you were going to marry Ridgeman within an hour of our first meeting. I had no reason to believe you'd change your mind."

"Yes, you did. You had every reason to think I had changed my mind. We made love only hours before West proposed. Our bodies made promises that I'm sure we both meant to honor. I meant to honor them, Ben, truly. I don't fall into bed with every man I find physically attractive. In fact, you're the first in...well, in a long time."

"You don't owe me an explanation, Sara."

"Yes, I do. I just don't have one to offer. What happened between us shouldn't have happened." Her eyes were clear as she held his gaze. "Even if West hadn't proposed this morning, I would still feel that way. You and I don't have a future together, Ben. You're not part of my plans. I'm sorry."

There was only one argument he could raise to refute her words, and he employed it with desperate resolve, covering the space between them in long strides, pulling her into his arms, taking her lips in a long and searching kiss.

Her response was instant and indisputable, but she pulled away and denied it with a lift of her chin and a flash of indignation in her eyes. "That isn't a proper way to kiss another man's bride."

"My mistake. I thought I was kissing you."

"Don't go away angry, Ben."

"Just go away?" He was angry. At the father whose careless dreams had instilled this fear in her, at the mother who had left her with too much responsibility, at the plans she had made that shut him out. "Imagine my surprise, Sara. Until now, I prided myself on being a good sport. But I don't like losing. And I especially don't like losing for the wrong reasons. And most of all, I don't like losing you."

Her hands twisted as she stared at the ground, and when she lifted her eyes, he saw a suspicious shimmer in their depths. He hoped she would cry, give him an excuse to hold her one more time. But he didn't expect her to shed a single tear...and she didn't.

"I was never yours to lose, Ben."

"Is there anything I can say to change your mind?"

"Please don't try. I'm not like you. I can't believe in love at first sight. I can't live for this moment without worrying about the next one. I need some certainty about what tomorrow will bring. I need to know I'm safe."

"And you think marrying Ridgeman will ensure that?" It was the wrong thing to say, he realized, when she stiffened.

"If you intend to challenge my decision, be honest about it. Admit that you're not safe, that you're high risk and dangerous, that life with you would be precarious and uncertain."

"True," he agreed. "Everything you said is absolutely true. The trouble is, you'll find it's true with Ridgeman, as well. Safety is an illusion. Life is precarious and uncertain and unpredictable. For all your planning, Sara, you are as much at its mercy as I am."

"I don't think so."

"You're about to jump off another wall."

She shook her head. "No. This time I'm going through the gate, just the way I planned."

Despite the ache inside him, he smiled. "If you weren't so stubborn, I'm not sure I would love you as much."

"If you weren't so stubborn, you wouldn't think you loved me at all."

"Now that's where you're wrong. You've underestimated me from the very beginning. Maybe you ought to update that intuition of yours." He walked to the Harley and swung his leg over the seat. Reaching for the ignition key, he paused. "Sara? Would it make any difference if I told you my net worth?"

A sound somewhere between tears and laughter escaped her throat. "One hundred dollars and fifty cents."

He raised his eyebrows. "Did you look in my wallet?"

She shook her head. "Merely a lucky guess."

"Well, you were wrong. You still owe me the fifty cents."

"So I do." She shifted her weight from one foot to the other. "I'll get it, if you want to wait."

"Don't bother. I'd rather have you in my debt." He patted his leg. "Come on, Cleo. Let's get going."

The dog lingered at Sara's side, and Ben wondered if he should have tried reverse psychology on both of them. "All right," he conceded. "Stay, if you want to."

To his surprise, Cleo stayed.

Sara pulled on her collar. "Go on, Cleo. Ben's waiting for you."

The Lab looked at her but didn't move.

"She prefers to stay with you." He forced a smile. "An understandable choice."

A stricken expression wiped the color from Sara's face. "No, Ben. You can't leave her behind."

Ben slipped on the helmet and started the motorcycle, watching as Cleo pressed her head against Sara's leg and closed her eyes at the touch of Sara's hand on her ear.

"It isn't my decision to make." He shrugged, feeling the heaviness inside him turn cold and lonely. "She's your problem now," he said.

Lifting his hand in goodbye, he revved the engine and drove away.

Chapter Thirteen

Somewhere a harp was playing Mozart. The smell of roses pervaded the room with a subtle fragrance. Sara looked in the oval mirror and saw a bride who looked remarkably like her, auburn hair, dark eyes, a gown as white as hope and as elegant as the seed pearls and raw silk from which it had been crafted. In her hands she held a bouquet of rosebuds, white against dark green foliage. All trace of thorns had been removed, of course. No bride should prick her finger and bleed on her wedding day. Especially not Sara. Especially not today.

"You're going to have to do something about your lipstick," Gypsy announced, getting to her feet after smoothing the bridal train.

Sara leaned toward the mirror. "Is it the color? I have another tube somewhere in my bag."

"I don't think the color matters. It's the way it makes your mouth droop at the corners."

Exerting the effort to smile, Sara met her friend's gaze in the mirror. "Is that better?"

Gypsy shrugged. "It will have to do, I suppose. Too bad no one has invented a lipstick that makes you look happy even when you're not."

"I'm happy," Sara lied. "I've planned this day all my life. Everything is perfect."

"Great. I'll just go and check on Tad, make sure he's still asleep and doesn't need his mother."

"Sooner or later you're going to have to start calling the baby by his real name."

"I don't see why. Just because legally he's Kevin, Jr., doesn't mean I can't give him a nickname."

"You'll embarrass him one day by calling him Tadpole in front of his friends."

Gypsy's forehead wrinkled in a frown. "So what's your point? If he's old enough to object, he's old enough to be embarrassed. That's the way it is with mothers and their sons."

Sara smiled at the sage tone in her friend's voice. "I won't argue with your superior experience...all three weeks of it."

"Now, that's the way you should smile on your wedding day." She stepped forward, a round, curly-haired blonde in the dark green silk that designated a member of the wedding party. "It isn't too late to change your mind, you know. If you're not absolutely sure..."

"Don't be silly." Sara turned Gypsy toward the door. "Go check on little Kevin while I change my lipstick. There's only a few minutes left before Jason gives us our cue."

"Now, who would have thought that brother of yours would turn out to be so responsible?" Gypsy commented slyly. "Why I can remember when you didn't think he could be trusted to take out the trash, and in the three weeks you've been planning this wedding, he's suddenly become Mr. Ambition himself."

"He's come a long way," Sara admitted.

"And surprised the stuffing out of you." Gypsy grinned. "A just reward, I must say. I always said that Jason just needed you to have a little faith in him. Was I right or was I right?"

"You were right. Now go and check on the baby before it's time."

"The Big Moment." Gypsy wrinkled her nose and left.

Sara looked at herself in the mirror and wondered why she wasn't more excited. Her big moment was at hand.

The other bridesmaids were already in the vestibule. By this time, West and his groomsmen would be at the front of the church waiting with the minister. DeeNee would be stepping to the microphone to sing the first of two selections. Everything was in place, just the way Sara had always planned.

Since the day of West's proposal, she hadn't had a minute to think about anything except the wedding. The rush to the altar was his suggestion, based on the demands of his hectic schedule and the timing of an impending trial. It was either now or months from now. And, as West pointed out, she owned a business that specialized in getting things done.

So, with Jason's help, Sara had made it happen in three short weeks. Every detail exactly the way she wanted. Every aspect just the way she'd planned. With a sigh, she adjusted the veil and frowned at her reflection. She was happy. West was the right man to be her husband. She knew what to expect from him and she knew what he expected from her. They were a perfect match. Both ambitious, focused, organized and sure of what they wanted. Their life would be all she had imagined. Despite what some people thought, there was nothing wrong with being able to predict what tomorrow would bring.

She squinted at the mirror, trying to see her future, trying to imagine West standing behind her. When she had put on the other wedding gown, she had imagined everything from its compelling twinkle to the glimpse of a man sharing her reflection. And if she had imagined all that, why couldn't she force West's image into the mirror now? Why was it Ben's face she saw, Ben's smile that matched her own, Ben's solid body she wanted to stand beside her?

She had made the right choice, the safe choice. Ben didn't belong in this picture. Turning, Sara glided to the door, pausing only long enough to give Cleo a stern command. "Don't you dare get off that blanket, Cleo. You are not invited to the ceremony. Do you understand? Stay put."

The Lab wagged her tail. She had been a model of decorum since Ben left, and Sara attributed the change to the strict, no-nonsense attitude she used whenever she gave a command. West didn't fare so well, but then it was no secret that he didn't like dogs.

As she stepped from the room, she could hear DeeNee's soft alto voice singing the words of a song that suddenly sounded wrong. It was the right song, the one she had chosen, and DeeNee was performing it perfectly. So why did Sara feel as if she'd made a terrible mistake?

She moved quickly down a short hall to the vestibule, fighting the feeling that she was moving in slow motion. Something wasn't right. Something... Despite the protesting murmurs of the bridesmaids, she walked past them and stopped in the doorway. Everything was in place. The church was full of family and friends. The flowers were perfect. The candles were lit. DeeNee raised an eyebrow when she noticed Sara, but she continued to sing. West, the minister and the groomsmen looked at her with some slight surprise. A few of the guests turned, smiling curiously, as people did when something was out of sync.

Sara looked down the aisle that stretched between her and the future she had planned so carefully and realized she was the one out of sync. She hadn't waited for her cue. She had been so afraid something would go wrong, she'd almost made it a self-fulfilling prophecy. Stepping back hastily, she stepped on her train and fell flat on her butt, sending a thud like thunder echoing through the church.

In a second, she was surrounded by a sea of green silk and the concern of her bridesmaids. DeeNee's voice faltered, but she kept singing, even over the hushed babble of whispers flowing from the crowd to Sara's ears. She tried to scoot out of the doorway, only to find too many hands stretched to help her, too much green silk in her way. In a panic, she scrambled onto her knees and attempted to crawl out of the picture. Just as she felt the dress pull across her back with a loud ripping sound, Gypsy entered the disaster zone and gasped audibly.

"Sara!"

No whispers out here, Sara thought miserably.

"Did you faint?" Gypsy hurried forward, bending over to discover the problem, blocking the path and keeping Sara on all fours by her awkward positioning. "Are you all right?" Without waiting for a reply, Gypsy straightened and scanned the audience. "Is there a doctor in the house?"

Collapsing with a moan seemed like her best option, but Sara was made of heartier stuff and she made another attempt to get to her feet, grasping the back of Gypsy's dress for leverage... and tearing the back bow right off the green silk dress. Gypsy whirled around, unaware that her underwear was on display, and the other two bridesmaids moved back, obviously afraid Sara would reach for them next. She struggled to her knees, ripping her wedding gown even more and breaking several strands of seed pearls, which hit the hardwood floor with a clatter and rolled down the aisle.

DeeNee stopped singing, and as if he knew the song wasn't over, Brody began to howl from his secluded seat in Harry's lap. Cleo trotted out, tail wagging, to investigate the commotion. She paused to lick Sara's chin and then joined her voice with the pug's in a howling duet.

"Shut up, you mongrels." West stalked down the aisle and stood over Sara, who could only look at him. "What in the hell is going on back here?"

"You shouldn't talk like that in church," she answered. "It's sacrilegious."

"Oh, and your making a mockery of our wedding isn't?"

"You think I did this on purpose? I wanted everything to be perfect."

"Well, it's not perfect now," he snapped, offering her a hand up.

Cleo took exception to either the gesture or his tone of voice and began to bark. West stamped his foot in her direction, causing her to jump back and bark some more. Brody scrambled out of Harry's arms and raced down the aisle to lend Cleo his moral support. Guests moved restlessly in the church pews, some of them staring openly, some of them politely pretending not to notice.

"Shut up!" West yelled at the dogs, who of course ignored him and kept barking. He bent down, grabbed Sara's rosebud bouquet and threw it at Cleo.

The Labrador picked it up in her mouth and did several artful dodges past the ladies in green silk, who tried to take it away from her. Gypsy lunged for the dog, only to be knocked off her feet when Brody dashed between them.

Together, the dogs raced down the aisle with their prize, slipping and sliding on the length of white satin that covered the floor. The minister reached down to stop Cleo as she ran past, and being a rotund man, his hips hit the left candelabrum, knocking it over, scattering hot wax and a dozen lit candles, which in turn started a dozen small fires on and around the length of white satin. The groomsmen and two guests from the front rows scurried about, stomping out the flames, while the minister ran from the baptistery to the altar carrying water in a cup, tossing it on what was left of the fires.

At the far end of the aisle, Sara sank onto her heels, thinking how long it had taken her to plan every last detail—and how quickly chaos had won the day. It was then that she started to laugh, a bubbling, light-hearted laugh that spilled from her lips in a surprising stream of relief. Her amusement elicited a few hesitant titters from the guests and a black scowl from West.

"I don't see anything funny about this," he said. "And I certainly can't understand why you're laughing."

"No, I don't suppose you would." Looking at him, Sara admitted that he was far from perfect. He would undoubtedly make a fine husband—but not for her. She couldn't spend the rest of her life thinking that he looked scrawny without his clothes on. "I can't marry you, West. I've seen you without your briefs."

"What?" He extended his hand with a continuing frown. "Come with me. We'll go somewhere private and talk about... Will you please stop laughing?"

She tried, but relief welled inside her until she couldn't suppress it. Gypsy leaned over and whispered through a giggle, "Does this mean I don't have to sew that dumb bow back on my dress?"

"You don't think I'm going to sew all those seed pearls back onto this one, do you?"

"Sara, please," West said impatiently. "I want to talk to you, but not in front of a church full of people."

"This looks like as good a place as any," she replied. "Shoot."

He glanced over his shoulder. "Not here. This is not the place for the discussion I have in mind."

"It will have to do, West, because in an hour I'm going to be on a plane to California."

"Don't be absurd, Sara. We'll plan another wedding for a few months from now. After I've won my case."

"You're not listening. I'm not making any more wedding plans. I'm going to California. Today."

"Do you realize how ridiculous that sounds?"

"Not ridiculous," she corrected. "Impulsive. It sounds like someone who's about to jump off a fence into a bramble bush."

Gypsy joined in. "It sounds like someone who would put on a wedding dress because she saw it twinkle."

Sara smiled. "Yes, it does, doesn't it? It even sounds like someone who's finally realized she believes in love at first sight."

Gypsy sighed. "I love happy endings, and I'm so glad I don't have to cry at your wedding."

"She just said there wasn't going to be a wedding." West looked angry and confused at the same time. "Which, if you two don't stop that silly giggling and get up off the floor, will soon be quite obvious to everyone."

Tails wagging—although in Brody's case, it was more like the whole back end—the dogs traipsed down the aisle like newlyweds, and Cleo dropped the crushed, saliva-sopped bouquet in Sara's lap.

"Thank you, Cleo. I always wanted to catch a bridal bouquet." She wrapped her arms around the Labrador and whispered in her ear. "Let's go see Ben, what do you say?"

Cleo's answer was an all-over, head-to-tail shake of happiness.

FINDING BEN was the easy part. It took an entire day and thirteen phone calls, but Sara hadn't put together At Your Service without becoming something of a detective. It required patience and persistence, and she had to curtail her impulse to jump on the first flight out of town. But once she had an address, everything fell into place as neatly as if she'd been planning the trip for months.

But when she stopped the rental car outside a house fronted by an expanse of green lawn and palm trees and backed against the blue Pacific, her palms began to sweat. She double-checked the directions she'd gotten from a clerk at the hotel and matched them against the numbers on a decorative post next to the driveway. "This is the place," she said to Cleo. "Ben must be working for the owners."

Cleo pushed her nose out the open window, snuffling the breeze off the ocean. Her tail whipped from side to side like a metronome, as if she knew Ben was near.

"I know just how you feel." Sara was nervous and eager, hopeful and scared, anxious and excited. One minute she imagined Ben taking one look at her and dropping to his knees to propose marriage. The next minute she was afraid he'd take one look at her and say, "What was your name again?"

She parked in front of the house and tried not to be intimidated at the thought of walking up and ringing the doorbell. It was just a house, she thought. Impressive as hell, but still just a house. Someone would answer the door and tell her where she could find Ben. Maybe she shouldn't have parked in the drive. Maybe she should have driven around back. But, no, better to ask first.

Cleo started barking, joyous gulps of noise to match the rhythm of her wagging tail.

"Okay, okay." Sara took a deep breath. "I'll ring the doorbell and ask for Ben. You stay put."

When she pushed it, the doorbell chimed like a church bell, its tone long and deep. She glimpsed a tall shadow through the tinted glass of the door and straightened her shoulders.

"Hello," she said in a rush of nervous energy the very second the door opened. "I'm looking for Ben Northcross. I think he might work..." Her voice trailed off in surprise as she took a good look at the tall, thin man who stood before her. "Arthur?"

"Ms. Gunnerson, I presume?"

"Arthur," she repeated. "What are you doing here?"

"I am the butler. May I ask what you are doing here?"

"I came to find Ben. You remember him—well, of course you would since he must have gotten you this job." She tried to swallow at least some of her amazement. "He is here, isn't he?"

"He's working in the garage today, I believe. If you'll step inside, I'll tell him you're here."

"Oh, no, don't do that. I wouldn't want to get him in any trouble. I'll, uh, just go around." She turned, then looked back. "I can walk to the garage, can't I?"

Arthur's dour expression didn't alter. "I'd prefer that you did, although I suppose I could carry you."

She frowned, feeling suddenly more comfortable and somehow grateful for Arthur's familiar dry humor. "West was very annoyed after you left," she said.

"Mr. West was very annoyed before I left."

"He'll be really upset when he finds out you're out here working with Ben."

The butler almost smiled. "He isn't much of a *sport*, is he?"

"No. Not much of a sport at all." With a wave that was far more lighthearted than she felt, Sara walked to the car. "Will it be all right to let Cleo run loose for a few minutes?" She turned the question to Arthur, but when she looked back, the door was closed and she was on her own.

Cleo bounded out of the car as if she'd been confined half her life, and by the time Sara followed her around the corner of the house, the dog was out of sight. Chasing butterflies, probably. Sara only wished she could hand over the butterflies fluttering in her stomach. She shouldn't have come here. She should have called first. Or written. Given him a chance to say he never wanted to see her again. Too late now. Arthur knew she was here, and he'd tell. And she couldn't leave without Cleo. And . . .

Ben was here.

She looked up and saw him, standing in front of an open bay in a garage with several spaces. He stood very still, wiping his hands on a rag as he watched her approach. Sara's heart hammered in her rib cage with a frantic *kathunk, kathunk, kathunk*. What if he'd fallen in love at first sight with someone else? It had been three weeks since she'd told him he didn't fit in with her plans. He could have found someone else and married her on the spot.

"You're a long way from home, Mrs. Ridgeman."

At his words, Sara's fears melted into an impulse that sent her rushing into his arms with such force that she knocked him off his feet and fell with him to the ground. When they stopped rolling, he was on top and she took the opportunity to enjoy a little wiggle of familiarity.

"Hey," he said. "What's the idea?"

"I wanted to surprise you."

"You did."

"That's it?" she asked. "No lectures on safety? No advice on the right way to fall?"

His eyes darkened and he pushed up, bracing his weight on his hands. "I doubt your husband would approve."

"Forget about him." She wrapped her hands around his neck. "I have. He doesn't even exist."

"The invisible husband. How convenient." He peeled her hands from his neck and got to his feet. She lay looking up at him, thinking his hair was lighter, his eyes a deeper green, his body more solid, his face so handsome she wanted to kiss every inch of it.

"I suppose the two of you are out here to persuade Arthur to return to the fold." Ben slapped at the grease on his faded blue jeans. "I'll warn you that he's already making twice the salary you can afford."

"That doesn't surprise me, considering that I'm in debt up to the end of my nose. In fact—" she sat up and dug into the pocket of her grass-stained khaki shorts "—I came to give you this." Holding out her hand, she offered him a single, shiny quarter.

He took it from her, and just the brush of his fingertips across her palm sent her pulse into overtime, set her nerve endings on fire. "Where's the rest of it?" he asked. "As I recall, you owe me fifty cents."

"I'm keeping the other quarter, Ben. If you want it, you're going to have to twinkle at me."

"Sara..."

He seemed to be lost for words, so she helped him out. "You should have been at the wedding. I planned it so perfectly, right down to the last detail. And then all my plans fell apart."

"All of them?"

She nodded. "I jumped the gun and tore my dress, then I tore Gypsy's dress, then Cleo snatched my bouquet and the minister knocked over the candelabrum and nearly set the church on fire and people were stomping around, West was yelling, the dogs were barking. It was quite a spectacle."

"Sorry I missed it."

"I laughed until I cried."

A familiar gleam of humor appeared in his eyes. "Did someone use reverse psychology on you?"

"No. I just changed my mind."

"About?"

"Getting married." She put her hand to her forehead to shade her eyes from the sun, and maybe from Ben, as well. "I finally realized you were right all along. No matter how well I plan, life is going to be unpredictable. So I left West at the altar and rushed off to track you here... By the way, your credit-card company is sending you a new unexpired card this week. Be sure to switch it as soon as you get it, and... What was I saying?"

He took her hand and pulled her to her feet. "You were about to explain why you're here."

"I wanted to find out if I could fall in love at first sight... even if I wasn't under the spell of a magic wedding dress."

His smile curved with tender amusement. "I never delivered the dress," he said. "It's inside the house right now—just in case you want to put it on."

"I don't think that will be necessary." Her lips fairly ached with the need to feel his kiss. "There's a convincing twinkle in your eyes and... I'm sorry, but if you don't kiss me right now, I'm going to die."

"It'll cost you a quarter."

"I'll pay you on our fiftieth wedding anniversary, and not a moment before. Now, pucker up." She went up on tiptoe, looping her arms around his neck and pulling his head down to hers.

The kiss was as good as anything she had ever experienced in California—or anywhere else in the world. When he lifted his head and cupped her chin in his hands, she got lost in his eyes, drowned in the love she found there. "Will you marry me?" she asked.

"Right now?"

"Whenever you say. Just don't ask me to plan a wedding."

"Deal."

She sighed with happiness. "Did I mention that I'm desperately in love with you?"

"No."

"I am. I'm afraid you're stuck with me and Cleo, for better or worse."

"Well, you'll be stuck with Arthur, so I think it's an even trade."

"You mean you got a steady job here?" The future glowed suddenly and then dimmed. "You'll have to quit, Ben. At Your Service is just beginning to show a profit... which right now will have to go toward the purchase of a sprinkler system and a new van, but maybe in a couple of years, we can afford for you to go to architectural school. But I can't abandon my business and move out here. You'll have to go back with me. I'll find something for you to do."

"You could move At Your Service to California. Or you could let Jason take it over."

"He's in charge right now. You wouldn't believe the change that's come over him in the last three weeks. At the rate he's taken charge of the business, I'll probably be obsolete when I get back."

"So there's your answer. Let Jason take care of the business and let me take care of you."

"I wouldn't be good at that and you know it. I like to take care of myself and I have this impulsive need to do things my way." She sighed, concerned by this blemish on her plans. "So if you won't leave your job and I can't leave my business, what will we do? Commute?"

"I'll teach you to fly."

"I already know how. I buy a ticket."

He laughed. "Don't tell me a risk taker like you doesn't want to learn how to fly an airplane, like that." He pointed across the lawn to an airstrip and a small, twin-engine plane. "It's not quite as exciting as riding the Harley, but I think you'll like it."

She looked from the plane to the house to him. "What kind of job is this?"

"I live here, Sara. This is my home."

Her mouth fell open. "You own this?"

Ben shrugged. "I never said I needed a job."

"But you told me you were down on your luck, that you didn't have fifty cents to call your own."

"No, that's what you told me. I did warn you not to rely too heavily on your intuition."

"I... This is quite a surprise." She hesitated. "Maybe I could move the business out here."

"Maybe I'll think about studying architecture."

"Ben?"

"Yes?"

"Do you still want to marry me?"

"It's the one thing I'm planning on, Sara."

She stood on tiptoe to taste his kiss once more. "Guess what?" she said. "There just happens to be a wedding chapel fifteen miles from here, and the minister said he'd be there until seven-thirty."

"Sara," he said in mock dismay. "Don't tell me you've been making plans again. I'm surprised at you."

"You're going to be even more surprised when you find out what else I have planned for you."

"It's good to be us."

"It's perfect," she said as he gathered her into his arms. "I just love it when a plan comes together."

He's at home in denim; she's bathed in diamonds...
Her tastes run to peanut butter; his to pâté...
They're bound to be together

*for
Richer,
for
Poorer*

We're delighted to bring you more of the kinds of stories
you love in FOR RICHER, FOR POORER—where lovers
are drawn by passion...but separated by price!

In June watch for:

#634 *REBEL WITH A CAUSE*
By Kim Hansen

Don't miss any of the
FOR RICHER, FOR POORER
books—only from

MILLION DOLLAR SWEEPSTAKES

BRIDE'S BAY RESORT

UNLOCK THE DOOR TO GREAT ROMANCE AT BRIDE'S BAY RESORT

Join Harlequin's new across-the-lines series, set in an exclusive hotel on an island off the coast of South Carolina.

Seven of your favorite authors will bring you exciting stories about fascinating heroes and heroines discovering love at Bride's Bay Resort.

Look for these fabulous stories coming to a store near you beginning in January 1996.

Harlequin American Romance #613 in January
Matchmaking Baby by Cathy Gillen Thacker

Harlequin Presents #1794 in February
Indiscretions by Robyn Donald

Harlequin Intrigue #362 in March
Love and Lies by Dawn Stewardson

Harlequin Romance #3404 in April
Make Believe Engagement by Day Leclaire

Harlequin Temptation #588 in May
Stranger in the Night by Roseanne Williams

Harlequin Superromance #695 in June
Married to a Stranger by Connie Bennett

Harlequin Historicals #324 in July
Dulcie's Gift by Ruth Langan

Visit Bride's Bay Resort each month wherever Harlequin books are sold.

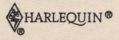

HARLEQUIN ®

BBAYG

HARLEQUIN®

AMERICAN ◆ ROMANCE®

With only forty-eight hours to lasso their mates—
it's a stampede...to the altar!

WILD WEST
Weddings

by Cathy Gillen Thacker

Looking down from above, Montana maven
Max McKendrick wants to make sure his heirs get
something money can't buy—true love! And if his two
nephews and niece want to inherit their piece of his
sprawling Silver Spur ranch then they'll have to wed the
spouse of *his* choice—within forty-eight hours!

Don't miss any of the Wild West Weddings titles!

#625 THE COWBOY'S BRIDE (April)

#629 THE RANCH STUD (May)

#633 THE MAVERICK MARRIAGE (June)

WWW

What do women really want to know?

Trust the world's largest publisher of
women's fiction to tell you.

HARLEQUIN ULTIMATE GUIDES™

I CAN FIX THAT

A Guide For Women
Who Want To Do It Themselves

This is the only guide a self-reliant
woman will ever need to deal
with those pesky items that
break, wear out or just don't work
anymore. Chock-full of friendly
advice and straightforward,
step-by-step solutions to the
trials of everyday life in our
gadget-oriented world! So, don't
just sit there wondering how to
fix the VCR—run to your
nearest bookstore for your copy now!

Available this May, at your favorite retail outlet.

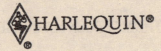

HARLEQUIN®

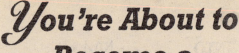

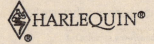